Anastasia's
Chosen Career

OTHER YEARLING BOOKS YOU WILL ENJOY:

YEARLING BOOKS/YOUNG YEARLINGS/YEARLING CLASSICS are designed especially to entertain and enlighten young people. Patricia Reilly Giff, consultant to this series, received her bachelor's degree from Marymount College. She holds a master's degree in history from St. John's University, and a Professional Diploma in Reading from Hofstra University. She was a teacher and reading consultant for many years, and is the author of numerous books for young readers.

For a complete listing of all Yearling titles, write to
Dell Readers Service, P.O. Box 1045,
South Holland, IL 60473.

Anastasia's Chosen Career

Lois Lowry

A Yearling Book

Published by
Dell Publishing
a division of
Bantam Doubleday Dell Publishing Group, Inc.
666 Fifth Avenue
New York, New York 10103

ISBN: 0-440-75296-5

Reprinted by arrangement with Houghton Mifflin Company

Printed in the United States of America

November 1988

10 9 8 7 6 5 4 3 2 1

RAD

This book and all of the books in this series are fictional. I made them up. I made up the people. I made up their names. Honest.

With that in mind, I would like to dedicate this one to several strangers:

Dr. M. Krupnick, from the University of Chicago, who wrote to me in 1981.

His wife, Kathryn Krupnick.

The Very Reverend Robert Giannini, Dean of the Cathedral Church of St. Peter, St. Petersburg, Florida, who wrote to me in 1985.

And lots of Anastasias.

Anastasia's
Chosen Career

1

"Everybody in the whole world skis, except me," announced Anastasia, as she reached for another helping of dessert. It was apple crisp, one of her favorites.

"*I* don't ski," said her brother, Sam, with his mouth full.

"Well, you're only three years old," Anastasia pointed out. "Everybody else skis."

Mrs. Krupnik, Anastasia's mother, wiped her mouth with a paper napkin. "Mr. Fosburgh, across the street, doesn't ski," she commented.

"Mr. Fosburgh has been in a wheelchair for thirty-four years," Anastasia said. "Everybody *else* skis."

Anastasia's father looked up. "I was just reading an article about tribespeople in the Kalahari Desert in Africa. It didn't mention that they ski."

Anastasia gave her entire family a look of disgust. It wasn't easy, because it meant that she had to maintain a look of disgust while turning her head slowly to focus first on Sam, then on her mother, then on her father.

"I *meant*," she said after a moment, after she had completed her look of disgust, "that it seems as if every-

1

one in my class skis. Everyone in the seventh grade. Winter vacation starts next week, and all my friends are disappearing. They're all going skiing."

"No kidding," her father said. "Everyone? Are they all going together? Why didn't they invite us?" He reached over and took some more apple crisp.

"No," Anastasia said gloomily. "Not all together. Daphne's going with her grandmother. Daphne's grandmother is taking her to Austria to ski. Can you imagine that? Daphne's grandmother skiing? She's *ancient!*"

"Well," Mrs. Krupnik said, "she's also extremely rich. Somehow extremely rich people seem to be able to do extremely amazing things."

"And Meredith," Anastasia went on. "Meredith's family isn't rich. But every single winter they go to New Hampshire to ski. They have these special ski outfits and everything. Meredith's is blue." Anastasia sighed, thinking about the blue skiing outfit Meredith Halberg had shown her. "It has snowflakes embroidered on the sleeves."

"I bet anything I could knit a sweater with snowflakes on the sleeves," Mrs. Krupnik said. "Remember I made that sweater for Sam last winter, with a cow across the chest? What ever happened to that sweater, Sam? You didn't lose it, did you?"

Sam shook his head. "It's under my bed," he said.

"Would you like me to make you a sweater with snowflakes on the sleeves, Anastasia?"

"*No*," Anastasia said, emphatically. Then she added, "Thank you, anyway."

2

Myron Krupnik took a third helping of apple crisp. "How about Steve Harvey?" he asked.

Anastasia groaned. "Steve Harvey is going with his father to Colorado because his father is covering some world championship ski races for NBC. Talk about *lucky*. I wish you were a sportscaster, Dad."

He laughed. "I think I'll stick with being a college professor and a poet. I don't know a soccer ball from a coronation ball. Anyway, even if I did, I could never be a sportscaster because I have arthritis in my neck and shoulders."

Anastasia stared at him. "So? What difference does that make? You could sit up straight and stare into a camera just fine. And they'd put powder over your bald spot so it wouldn't glisten. Maybe they'd even give you a toupee, if you were a sportscaster."

"My neck doesn't swivel. Picture me trying to announce a tennis match."

Anastasia pictured a tennis match, and she could see that her father was correct. You definitely needed a swivelly neck to announce a tennis match. Just her luck, to have a father with an unswivelly neck and a boring job.

Mrs. Krupnik stood up and began to collect the dessert plates. "Are you finished, Myron, or do you want to lick the bowl?"

Dr. Krupnik grinned and scraped the last invisible bits of apple crisp from his plate. Then he handed the empty plate to his wife.

Sam had climbed down from his chair and removed

3

his shoes. In his stocking feet, he ran suddenly across the dining room to the place where the rug ended, and slid across the wooden floor out into the hall. Anastasia and her parents could hear the crash as Sam ran into the wall and fell against a small table that had been piled with books. They heard the books hit the floor.

After a moment Sam came back into the dining room, rubbing his behind. "I was skiing," he explained. "But it wasn't that much fun."

Anastasia trudged up the stairs to her third-floor bedroom after *The Cosby Show* ended. She wondered if Bill Cosby's family went skiing, and decided that they probably did. It sure was boring, living in a family that never did anything truly exciting, especially during school vacations. Sometimes they went to the New England Aquarium. Big deal: penguins and turtles. Sometimes they went to the Museum of Science. Big deal: exhibits about friction and gravity, two of the most boring things in the world. Sometimes they went to the Museum of Fine Arts. Big deal: paintings, and statues of naked people, usually with their more interesting parts crumbled.

In her room, Anastasia first did the thing she almost always did every evening. She sat in front of the mirror and stared at herself. She gathered up her hair in one hand and tried to arrange it in various styles. First she gathered it into a big ball on top of her head. Then she tried it pulled entirely to one side, hanging down beside her left ear. Next, she parted it in the middle and pulled it into two ponytails, one on either side of her head. Each time, she sighed, staring at her reflection, and let her hair drop again into its ordinary thick, shoulder-length mass.

She pushed her glasses down farther on her nose and pursed her lips into a tight, refined look. She stared at herself and decided that she looked like a schoolmistress from the nineteenth century. Then she pushed her glasses back up where they belonged and tried a broad, toothy smile. She turned sideways, flung her head back, and looked at herself out of the corners of her eyes. She moved her shoulder forward, turned her neck — *her* neck swiveled, at least — and sucked in her cheeks, although it meant that she couldn't smile. She pulled some hair over her face and tugged at the neck of her sweat shirt until one shoulder was exposed. There. She held that pose, her favorite, for a moment. She liked it: haughty, disheveled, devil-may-care, flagrant. Anastasia liked the idea of being *flagrant*, even though she wasn't exactly sure what the word meant.

She stood up and wandered over to her unmade bed where her school books were strewn. She flipped through her history book, glanced at her homework paper, and decided she'd done enough, even though she'd answered only ten questions out of the twelve. She could do the other two in study hall before history class.

Anastasia lay down on her bed, wiggling a little to keep the corner of her notebook from poking her in the back, and thought about the coming week-long vacation from seventh grade. She had absolutely nothing to do during vacation except to work on her school project: a paper called "My Chosen Career."

Gross. How could you write about My Chosen Career when you hadn't even chosen one yet? Worse: all the seventh-graders were supposed to interview a person already working in their chosen career. Meredith was going to cheat; she was going to interview the owner of the ski lodge where her family always stayed. Then she was going to pretend that she wanted to own a ski lodge when she grew up.

Steve Harvey was going to interview his own father, for pete's sake. Talk about *easy*.

Daphne had already interviewed the guy her mother worked for, and now she was pretending that she wanted to be a lawyer. What a fake. Everybody *knew* that Daphne wanted to be an actress when she grew up. But Anastasia could sympathize with Daphne's problem; Daphne had written letters to Katharine Hepburn, Debra Winger, and Joanne Woodward, asking for interviews. All she got back were autographed pictures, and the autographs weren't even real — when you licked your finger and tried to smear them, they didn't smear at all.

It really wasn't entirely true, that *everyone* was going skiing. Daphne was going to Austria with her grandmother; that was true. They were flying from Boston tomorrow, and Daphne got to miss a whole day of school. Meredith's family really was going to New Hampshire, as they always did. And Steve Harvey was leaving for Colorado with his father on Sunday.

But Sonya Isaacson — one of Anastasia's very best friends — would be around. The Isaacson family didn't ski, maybe because every one of them was a little bit plump, Anastasia thought; maybe that would make skiing difficult.

Anastasia wasn't plump at all. I am *slender*, she thought, and held up one arm to look at it, hoping it would look long-limbed and graceful. Long-limbed and graceful my foot, she thought. I'm *bony*. Skinny and bony. *Tall* and skinny and bony. And my hair is gross. My posture is disgusting. I'm nearsighted. I have a chicken-pox scar on my forehead, and I hate my nose.

Even if my parents bought me a pale blue skiing outfit and took me to New Hampshire — no, took me to *Austria* — I would still be me, Anastasia thought. I would still be a tall, skinny, bony, gross-haired, slump-shouldered, nearsighted, big-nosed freak of a person.

She pictured a gorgeous, tan, blond ski instructor named — what? Hans. He would be named Hans. He would be wearing goggles pushed up over his blond hair and a black turtleneck sweater, she decided. His ski pants would be skintight, and she would be able to see the rippling muscles in his long, slim, ski instructor legs. His even white teeth would gleam in the Austrian sunshine. He would smile at her — gleam, gleam, gleam. And he would say in a deep, masculine, ski instructor voice —

Anastasia groaned aloud. She knew *exactly* what he would say. And he would say it in a sexy, ski instructor, Austrian accent, which made it even worse.

He would say, "Young lady, you vill have to leave dis mountain immediately. Ve don't allow skinny, bony, nearsighted, big-nosed people to come to ski slopes. Go back to Boston and improve yourself."

Anastasia sat up. That did it. A *daydream* did it: made a decision for her.

"Thanks, Hans," she said. "You've forced me to face reality." She reached over to the drawer of the table beside her bed. On the table, in his bowl, her goldfish looked at her with amazed eyes.

"Don't bug me, Frank," Anastasia said to her goldfish. "Just don't bug me."

She opened the drawer and took out the piece of paper that had been stored there for several months, ever since the day it had appeared under the windshield wiper of her father's car when they came out of the Paris Cinema after seeing a Woody Allen movie.

With the paper in her hands, she opened the door to her room and called down the stairs.

"Mom? Dad?"

No answer. Far below, on the first floor, she could hear the television. They were watching *Hill Street Blues*, their favorite TV show.

Anastasia went down to the second floor, tiptoed past the bedroom door where Sam was sleeping, and then went partway down the stairs to the first floor. She sat down on the stairs, pressed her face against the railing, and called into the study.

"Mom? Dad?"

Her mother came into the hall from the study and

8

looked up at Anastasia. "What?" she asked.

"Mom," Anastasia said, "you said that you and Dad would talk over what I asked you, about going in to Boston all by myself on the bus during school vacation. Did you? Did you talk it over?"

Sounds of gunshots came from the television. Mrs. Krupnik was standing there, but it was obvious to Anastasia that her mother hadn't even listened to her question. Her mother was listening to the television. Talk about supportive parents.

"To take that course, Mom. Remember?"

"Katherine!" Dr. Krupnik called urgently. "They've taken Bobby Hill hostage!"

"Go on back, Mom," Anastasia said with a sigh. "I'll discuss it with you at breakfast."

Anastasia read the paper again as she wandered back up to the third floor to get ready for bed. She had had it memorized for several weeks, but still she read the words over and over.

"Frank?" she said. She looked over at her goldfish. Frank opened and closed his mouth several times, very slowly. If Frank could talk, Anastasia thought, he would say nothing but "Oh. Oh. Oh."

"Frank," Anastasia told him, "if my parents will let me go all by myself into Boston on the bus during school vacation next week — "

Frank flipped his translucent tail and executed a languid somersault through the water.

"And they'd *better* let me, because I'm old enough — I'm thirteen, after all — well, then my school vacation

9

isn't going to be at all boring. Because I'm going to do something absolutely incredible! And educational, too. And to prepare me for my chosen career: how about *that*, Frank?"

Frank stared at Anastasia and moved his mouth again. "Oh. Oh. Oh," he said silently, as if maybe he knew something that she didn't.

Anastasia sighed, opened her notebook, and began to work on her school project.

My Chosen Career

After a great deal of careful thought about my
future, I have chosen a career which will be exciting,
glamorous, and

2

Mrs. Krupnik shook her head apprehensively. Her hair was tied back with a piece of yellow yarn, and she was wearing her plaid bathrobe.

"I don't know, Anastasia. Dad and I *have* talked about it, and we don't entirely agree. It really sounds risky to me. Sam, quit playing with your eggs. *Eat* them, please."

"I'm making a mountain," Sam said. He piled another forkload of scrambled eggs on top of the mound he'd fashioned on his plate. "When it's all made, then my fork will ski down. *Then* I'll eat it."

Mrs. Krupnik looked at her watch. "Sam, your car-pool driver will be here in ten minutes. Think of all the exciting stuff you're going to do at nursery school this morning. Eat your breakfast."

Carefully Sam reached over to the sugar bowl, took a spoonful of sugar, and sprinkled it on top of his scrambled-egg mound. "Snow," he said happily. "Snow on my skiing mountain."

Anastasia carried her own empty plate to the kitchen sink. "*Mom*," she said, "I am thirteen years old. Practically adult. What's risky about a practically adult person going alone to Boston on the bus in broad daylight?"

Mrs. Krupnik frowned and sipped her coffee. "I keep remembering what that guy says at the beginning of *Hill Street Blues*. He gives everybody their assignments, and then he looks very solemn, and he says —" She took another sip of coffee. "Myron, what does he say when he sends them all out after roll call?"

Dr. Krupnik looked up from the newspaper. " 'Remember,' " he said in a serious voice, " 'Be very, very careful out there.' "

"Right." Mrs. Krupnik picked up a piece of toast and began to spread some raspberry jam on it. "There's all sorts of crime and violence in cities, Anastasia." She looked over at Sam. "*Sam!* Stop it!"

Sam was sprinkling more and more sugar on his egg mountain. "Blizzard," he said blissfully.

Anastasia tried very hard to be patient and reasonable, because she knew that if they got into a big argument she would lose. "Mom," she said, "and Dad. I *am* a very, very careful person. I've been in Boston a million times, with you guys. I know my way around. I don't ever speak to strangers. The bus goes right to the corner of Tremont Street and I'd only have to walk two blocks. It would be daylight. They said on the news that the mayor has cracked down on the drug dealers in Boston Common—"

"The *what?*" Mrs. Krupnik asked in an astonished voice.

Whoops. That had been a mistake, mentioning drug

13

dealers, Anastasia realized. Parents wanted to think that thirteen-year-old people had never heard about drug dealers.

"Actually," Anastasia said hastily, "I was referring to last summer, when there was a small problem with crime in the city. But now the mayor has solved that.

"And you know," she went on slyly, changing her tactics a little, "I have this very important school project to work on. So this will give me a chance to do the research."

"Research?" her father asked, looking up from his paper with interest. "For school?" There was nothing her father liked more than the thought of one of his children doing research for school.

Mrs. Krupnik looked at her watch again. She got up and went to get Sam's winter jacket, which was hanging on a hook by the back door. "Sam," she said, "you now have about three minutes until your ride comes."

Sam aimed his fork into the top of his sugar-and-egg mountain, pried off a large forkful, and put it into his mouth. He made a terrible face. "I hate my eggs," he said.

Mrs. Krupnik sighed. "Here, Sam," she said. She handed him the half slice of toast she had left. "Eat this." She helped Sam into his jacket, pulled a woolen hat down over his curls, and thrust his mittens into his pockets. "There's Mrs. Harrington now, beeping her horn. Goodbye. See you at lunch." She closed the back door behind Sam and they all watched from the window as he

14

climbed into the back seat of the nursery school car.

"Now *I* only have ten minutes before I have to leave," Anastasia said. "Please, Mom. Please, Dad. I really want to do this. And I have to make the phone call this afternoon."

"Anastasia, it is *so* much money," said her mother. "Your dad and I were hoping that after your summer job, after you put all that money in the bank, you would develop some sense of financial responsibility — you know, looking ahead to the future."

Anastasia tried to be patient. "Mom, I *told* you that this would be in preparation for a career. It would be *educational*."

"Well," said Mrs. Krupnik. "Myron, what do you think?"

"I like the idea of school research," Dr. Krupnik said. "I wish *my* students would do research during vacations. What kind of research would you be doing?"

"My Chosen Career," Anastasia reminded him.

Her father's face brightened. "That's right," he said. "I forgot that you had that assignment. You were thinking about Bookstore Owner. I think that's a terrific idea."

"Actually," Anastasia told her father, "I've kind of changed my mind about Bookstore Owner. Now, since I want to take this course, I'm thinking more along the lines of — "

But her father was already reaching for the telephone book. "Let me check the address," he said. "There's a wonderful little bookstore on Beacon Hill, and I met the

15

owner when my last book of poetry came out. She had a wine-and-cheese party there at the store, and an autographing."

"Dad," Anastasia said, "I've been thinking that—"

"Only three people actually bought the book," he muttered. "Forty-seven people came and forty-seven people drank wine and ate cheese, but only three bought the book. Still, she was a nice woman."

"Myron," Mrs. Krupnik said, "she could interview a bookstore owner right here in town. She doesn't have to go all the way into the city for that."

"Here it is," Dr. Krupnik said, with his finger on one of the yellow pages. "Mount Vernon Street. That's a good safe part of the city, if she goes in the daytime."

"Myron," said Mrs. Krupnik again. "She could go right down the street. There's a Waldenbooks right down the street."

"Mom," Anastasia pointed out, "there are a million Waldenbooks all over the country. Mr. Walden probably lives in New York or something. And what I need is a bookstore owner, if I'm going to do Bookstore Owner for My Chosen Career."

"Oh," said Mrs. Krupnik. "You're right."

"Anyway," Anastasia went on, "it's really the *other* thing that I want to do in Boston. It would be *so* self-improving," Anastasia exclaimed. "And I *need* self-improvement. Even if I were going to be a bookstore owner, I would need self-improvement."

Dr. Krupnik was dialing. "I hope she remembers me," he said. "Do you think a bookstore owner remembers someone whose book sold only three copies?"

But the bookstore owner did. She remembered him, and she said that she would be willing to be interviewed by Anastasia.

"At noon," Anastasia whispered to her father while he was on the phone. "At lunchtime. Because I'm going to be doing this *other* thing, too."

"Here you are," her father said after he had hung up. He handed Anastasia a slip of paper. "Her name and the address of the store. She'll see you at twelve-fifteen on Monday. She said you could have a sandwich with her, there in the shop, while you do the interview."

Anastasia looked at it. "So now I'm going to be a Bookstore Owner," she said.

"Right," her father told her, grinning. "And you'll have wine-and-cheese parties and autographings for poets. For your dad."

Anastasia folded the paper. "Well, if I promise to do that — and I promise to sell more than three copies — can I do the other thing, *please?*"

"Oh, all right," her father said. "At least it will keep you busy during vacation. It seems like a harmless enterprise to me. Katherine, what do you think?"

"Well," Mrs. Krupnik said dubiously, "okay."

Anastasia jumped up and hugged each of them. "Thank you!" she said. "I have such great parents! Greater than anybody's! You know what Sonya's parents said when she asked them if *she* could do it? They said it was incredibly low class and tacky and revolting and expensive and absolutely ridiculous. What do *they* know, right?"

17

* * *

"They're really letting you do it?" Sonya held her large notebook in front of her face so that Mr. Earnshaw wouldn't see that she was whispering. They were in study hall. "*Really?*"

Anastasia, behind her notebook, nodded. "I'm going to call this afternoon."

"How're you going to pay for it? It costs a fortune!" Sonya peered up to the front of the room, but Mr. Earnshaw was busy at his desk, correcting papers.

"Out of my savings account. I have the money I earned last summer — remember I worked for Daphne's grandmother? And also I have the money that my aunts and uncles send on my birthday every year; my parents always make me put it in the bank. So I have about three hundred dollars in my savings account. And this only costs a hundred and nineteen. Shhhh." Anastasia ducked her head and pretended to read her history book. Mr. Earnshaw had stood up and begun to prowl around the room.

After he had passed her desk and observed her diligently reading about the Battle of Bull Run, Anastasia unfolded the piece of paper and read it for the billionth time.

INCREASED POISE, it said at the top.

Boy, thought Anastasia, I can sure use *that*. I have zero poise.

She remembered all the times that she had *needed* poise and it hadn't been there. The time, just recently, for example, when on Careers Day at the junior high,

18

Anastasia had been assigned to guide the lady architect around the corridors of the school as she visited classes. Anastasia had practiced the night before, things she might say to an architect — *poised* things — and then, when she tried to say them, when she began, "Architecture interests me a great deal. My family lives in a Victorian house that was built in — " she had walked right smack into a glass door, practically wrecking her nose.

She was still embarrassed thinking about it, even though the lady architect had been very sympathetic and kind and had given her a Kleenex to hold against her fat lip, which bled a little.

INCREASED CONFIDENCE, the paper said.

And if anybody needed increased confidence, it was Anastasia. If she'd had enough confidence, she would have run for Class Secretary. She really *wanted* to be Class Secretary. She really liked taking minutes. She liked the *word* "minutes." She wanted to write "Minutes" at the top of a page and then take notes. She would have done it better than anybody — certainly better than stupid old Emily Ewing, who had so much confidence that she had not only run for Class Secretary but had made posters that said

EXTRAORDINARY EXCELLENCE
EMILY EWING

and everybody voted for her. But Emily always forgot to go to the meetings. She only wanted to be Class Secretary because she wanted her picture in the yearbook. Anastasia would have been a much better Class Secretary, but she hadn't had the confidence.

19

Soon I will, Anastasia thought with satisfaction.

She read the final phrase at the top of the paper. INCREASED MATURITY.

It didn't seem as important as poise and confidence. Anastasia's parents assured her often that she was very mature for thirteen. She read mature books, watched mature programs on TV, behaved in a mature way, not whining and fooling around the way her brother did. Sometimes she *sulked*, true; but mature people sulked now and then. Her mother had sulked all evening the time that she spent hours making a casserole with a whole lot of fancy ingredients and then practically no one in the family would eat it. Anastasia had started to eat it, until she found out that it contained liver, which she hated. Her father had started to eat it, until he saw an artichoke heart, which he hated. Sam ate it, because Sam ate just about anything, but Mrs. Krupnik had sulked anyway. Anastasia had acted very maturely on that occasion, going to the kitchen to make peanut butter and jelly sandwiches for herself and her father.

It was the small print, farther down, that Anastasia really liked; and she read it now, again and again.

videotaping
hair styling
make-up instruction
posture clinic
voice modulation
diet modification
fashion consultation

She wasn't quite sure what "modification" or "modulation" meant. But since the whole $119 week was called "Junior High Models Workshop," she figured that they had to do with modeling. Weird. Maybe you modeled clothes and modificated your diet and moduled your voice. She would learn about all that stuff when she took the course.

Of course, if she became a fashion model, there would be a whole new set of problems, Anastasia realized. She propped up her notebook again, ducked her head, and whispered, "Sonya?"

Sonya lifted her notebook and looked over from her desk. "What?"

"Would you pose for nude photographs if they asked you?" Anastasia whispered.

"New photographs? Of course. Especially if I lost weight. I'd throw my *old* photographs away. They're all *fat*."

"Not new. *Nude*," Anastasia whispered.

Sonya looked puzzled. "*Noon* photographs?" she asked.

"*NUDE*," Anastasia said aloud.

Everyone in the study hall burst out laughing. Mr. Earnshaw stood up, straightened his glasses, and aimed his eagle eyes at Anastasia.

"Anastasia Krupnik," he said, "I'll speak to you here at my desk privately, as soon as the bell rings." Then he smiled a pinched, sarcastic smile. "Fully clothed, of course," he added.

Blushing, Anastasia began to arrange her books. Poise and confidence: she thought hard, willing those two

21

qualities into herself as she prepared to explain to Mr. Earnshaw. Poise and confidence.

"I have to confess I'm a little nervous about modeling school," Anastasia said to her parents that night. Sam was in bed, and they were sitting in the study in front of the fireplace. Her father had put one of his favorite records on the stereo. His eyes were closed, and he was directing the music with his hands in the air.

"Ta da dum, ta da dum," he sang softly, with the record. "Hear that phrasing? Mozart was a genius."

Anastasia nodded politely, even though her father still had his eyes closed and couldn't see her. He was so weird when he got involved with Mozart. Her mother just smiled and continued knitting.

Anastasia didn't know a single kid who knit, or who listened to Mozart. She wondered how those things came about. Did you wake up one morning, suddenly, at age seventeen or so, with a sudden urge to knit mittens? And when did Mozart happen? Her father had once told her that he had loved the Beatles when he was young. What had gone wrong? Had he, years before, maybe when he was in college, had an overwhelming desire one day to turn off *Sergeant Pepper* and replace it with a symphony? She would have to ask him. But not, she knew, while the record was playing.

"Of course you're nervous," her mother was reassuring her. "You were nervous when you began your job last summer. You were nervous the first day of school.

Everybody's nervous when they set out on a new venture."

"Actually," Anastasia reminded her, "I have *two* new ventures going on at the same time. When I go to Boston, I'm not only going to go to the modeling course; I'm also going to do the Bookstore Owner interview. . . ."

Her mother looked at her warily. "Anastasia, *promise* us that you will go directly to the bookstore. And to the modeling course. And to and from that bus. No fooling around in the city."

"Fooling around? *Moi?*"

The music stopped, and Dr. Krupnik stood up to turn the record over. "I want you to listen carefully to the third movement," he said.

"Myron," Anastasia's mother said, "do you have any advice for Anastasia about the interview?"

"You could ask her why my book sold only three copies in her store," he suggested.

"Ha ha," Anastasia said sarcastically. "I wouldn't ask something like that. It's important to be super-polite during the interview. We have this sheet of instructions. Also we're supposed to ask open-ended questions."

"What's an open-ended question?" asked Mrs. Krupnik.

Anastasia remembered the instructions their class had been given. "Well," she explained, "if you just ask, 'Do you like being a bookstore owner?' she could just say yes or no. And it would be boring. So, instead, you ask, 'What exactly do you like about being a bookstore owner?'

Then she has to *say* something. That's an open-ended question."

Her father frowned. He was holding the arm of his stereo turntable carefully in his hand. "Now pay attention, you guys. This third movement is incredible," he said.

"Dad," Anastasia asked, "what exactly do you like about Mozart? That's an open-ended question."

"Shhhhh," said her father.

My Chosen Career

After a lot of careful thought, I have decided that for my chosen career I am going to be a bookstore owner. To be a bookstore owner it is necessary to have increased poise and self-confidence. So as part of the educational requirements it is probably a good idea to take a modeling course.

The bus will be late, Anastasia thought, stamping her feet in the snow. I know the bus will be late. The bus will be late, and then I will be late, and I'll be the only person in the whole class who is late. How humiliating. They'll probably kick me out, before I ever start. And they'll make me pay the money anyway. I'll have to pay the whole $119, and they won't even let me take the course because I'm late the first day.

But then she heard the hiss of brakes and looked up, and the bus was there.

Waiting in line behind a lady who had to wrestle two small children up the slippery bus steps, Anastasia looked at her watch.

I'm going to be early, she thought. Good grief. I'm going to be a whole half hour early. I'll be the first one there, and they'll all laugh at me. How humiliating. The earliest one there. You're not *eager* or anything, Krupnik?

The bus lurched, starting up, and Anastasia stumbled toward an empty seat after paying her fare. I hope this is

26

the right bus, she thought nervously. What if I got on the wrong bus? What if this bus is headed to New York or something? Oh, great. I should have asked the driver if this was the right bus.

She looked toward the front and studied the back of the bus driver's head. He was a middle-aged man with a mustache, and he was staring straight ahead as he drove, squinting against the bright sunlight reflected off the snow.

That looks like a New York bus driver, Anastasia decided. I am on the wrong bus. Good grief, I am going to New York. I always *wanted* to go to New York someday, but I sure didn't want to go to New York all by myself, wearing jeans. How will I get home?

"You going shopping?"

Anastasia was startled when the woman beside her spoke. She glanced over at an elderly woman in a tweed coat, clutching a fat green pocketbook in her lap.

"Excuse me?"

"I asked if you were going shopping. I'm going to Filene's Basement. I go to Filene's Basement every day. The only way you can get bargains is to go every single day. Are you headed for Filene's?"

That was a relief. Filene's was in downtown Boston, so she was on the right bus. Anastasia shook her head and smiled politely at the lady. She had promised her mother and father that she wouldn't speak to strangers, but she figured that shaking her head and smiling politely was okay.

The woman kept on talking. "Half the people on this

27

bus are going to Filene's Basement. Right now you see them all in coats and hats, right? Half an hour from now, they'll all be standing around Filene's Basement in their underwear."

Anastasia stared at her. "I beg your pardon?" she asked.

"No dressing rooms," the woman explained. "So you have to try things on right out in the open. That woman over there — you see her, in the blue hat? She always wears two slips, one on top of the other."

Anastasia blinked her eyes and looked straight ahead. Ten minutes after I promise my parents that I won't talk to strangers, she thought, and here I am involved in a conversation about underwear.

"So," the woman continued, while she opened her pocketbook, took out a compact, opened it, and examined her lipstick in the mirror, "are you going shopping?"

"No," Anastasia said uncomfortably, "I'm going to modeling school."

The woman snapped the compact closed. "Oh," she said, "Of course. I should have guessed."

"Guessed? Why?"

"Because you're tall," the woman said. "And thin."

Anastasia slouched down in the bus seat gloomily. Thanks a lot, she thought. You *could* have said "because you have such great cheekbones."

The woman droned on and on, talking about the bargains in Filene's Basement, but Anastasia stopped listening. She began to picture herself at the end of the week, getting on this same bus Friday afternoon, maybe sitting beside this same lady. Ha. The woman would look exactly the same — green pocketbook, frizzy gray hair — but Anastasia would be entirely different. Tall, yes. Thin, yes. But poised, confident, with — she thought about the small print on the paper — a new hair style, a modified diet, better posture, a moduled voice, and an entirely revised sense of fashion.

She remembered that it had said make-up, also. Anastasia had never worn make-up. Well, not *really*. Occasionally she had *tried* wearing make-up, but it never seemed to work. She didn't seem to have the hang of it. But of course modeling school would teach her that.

Now the bus was entering the city. Anastasia peered through the grimy window and watched the tall buildings pass. She watched all the poised, confident people striding briskly along the sidewalks. Soon she would be one of them — well, not *that* one, she thought, as she spied an obese woman waddling along, bellowing at a small child scurrying by her side.

She reached into her pocket and pulled out the yellow slip of paper on which her father had written the address of the bookstore and its name: PAGES.

What a neat name for a bookstore, Anastasia thought: *Pages.* The owner had probably agonized for hours and hours before she thought of the perfect name.

Anastasia thought about some questions she could ask the owner.

"Was it fun, choosing just the right name for your bookstore?"

No. That wasn't open-ended. The owner could just say, "Yes."

Anastasia tried to rephrase the question. "What thinking process did you go through, choosing just the right name for your bookstore?" There. That was just right.

Maybe, she realized, in order to be super-polite, she ought to include the woman's name in the question. "What thinking process did you go through, choosing just the right name for your bookstore, Ms. — " She looked again at the paper and read the name of the owner.

BARBARA PAGE.

Oh. Well, maybe she *hadn't* agonized for hours and hours before she thought of the perfect name for her bookstore.

The bus slid to a stop and interrupted Anastasia's thoughts. They were here: downtown Boston. She could see the Boston Common on one side of her and the State House, with its gold dome, beyond.

She waited while the people around her stood and made their way to the front of the bus: women, mostly, with shopping bags, umbrellas, and pocketbooks. They looked like housewives, grandmothers, schoolteachers; Anastasia found it hard to believe that within a few minutes they would all be standing around Filene's Basement in their underwear.

"Excuse me, dear." The woman beside her shoved past and hurried off. Anastasia followed.

She had to walk two blocks to the modeling school. Anastasia hitched up her jeans, smoothed her parka, and adjusted her posture — she had been trying since Friday to remember good posture. The evening before, with her parents, she had examined a street map of Boston. With her finger she had traced the direction she would walk. Now she got her bearings and started off.

She wondered what the modeling school would look like. Of course, she had a pretty good idea from TV movies. There would be a tasteful bronze sign attached to the wall beside the front door. Inside, there would be soft carpeting — gray, she thought, or beige — with some colorful cushions, maybe red or yellow, strewn on the soft couches in the waiting room. The lights would be bright, and there would be a gorgeous receptionist in designer clothes at a big semicircular desk. Phones would be ringing constantly. In the background, music would be playing.

She turned a corner and passed a Chinese fast-food place and a typewriter repair shop. A young woman standing beside the typewriter place was stamping her feet to warm them and saying something to people who passed by.

"Got a quarter? Spare a quarter?" the woman asked Anastasia as she walked past.

Anastasia shook her head as the other people had done. She felt a little guilty, because she *did* have a quarter, and she could probably spare it, too. But she had noticed that the woman was wearing L. L. Bean boots. Anastasia knew what those cost, and she was pretty certain that someone who could afford L. L. Bean boots didn't need to scrounge quarters.

31

Still, she thought, maybe the woman had *found* the boots someplace. Maybe she was really, truly hungry. Maybe she had small starving children. . . .

Anastasia hesitated. She turned and looked back at the young woman again. A man had stopped and was dropping some change into her outstretched hand. Then he walked on. The woman pocketed the money, glanced at Anastasia, grinned, and winked.

Anastasia stared at her in astonishment. Then she readjusted her posture and headed on toward the end of the block, checking the numbers on the buildings.

365. 367. 369. That was it: 369. But it didn't look right. She took the paper out of her pocketbook and checked: 369. It *was* right. But there was no tasteful bronze sign. There was a jewelry store, its window filled with gold chains and plastered over with hand-written signs: CLOSE-OUT. EVERYTHING MUST GO. GOING OUT OF BUSINESS. 50% OFF.

To the left of the jewelry store entrance was another door, a windowed door with peeling gilt letters. TUDI HARM NTE, they said. Anastasia wiped the moisture from her glasses and looked again. Now she could make out the places where the gold paint had faded and peeled, and she could read what they were intended to say.

STUDIO CHARMANTE

That was it. "Studio Charmante" was what it said at the top of the paper advertising the modeling course. Anastasia gulped, and opened the door.

* * *

Inside, a dark staircase loomed. A handwritten sign was Scotch-taped to the wall beside the stairs. STUDIO CHARMANTE, 2ND FLOOR was scribbled on it, and an arrow pointed up.

Anastasia hesitated. The stairs were very dark, and the pale green paint on the walls was dirty and flaked. She squinted in the dim light and looked at her watch; it was 9:15 and the modeling course was scheduled to begin at 9:30. So she had fifteen minutes to make a decision.

She could go back home, she realized. But she would miss lunch with the bookstore owner, and she would miss her interview with the bookstore owner, and her school project would be wrecked. And she would have to explain to her parents, and to Sonya, and it would be so humiliating.

She could — but her thoughts were interrupted when the door behind her opened. Anastasia jumped and turned, terrified, prepared to face a mugger, a murderer, a person demanding spare quarters.

But it was a girl her own age: a pretty black girl wearing jeans, sneakers, a bright red jacket, and a disgusted look. She was holding a paper in her hand, the same paper that Anastasia held.

"This sure don't look like no modeling school," the girl said loudly. "It looks like Cockroach City."

"I know," Anastasia replied. "I was scared to go up."

"Appears to me we got choices," the girl said. "My choice is, I go upstairs and check things out for a week in this here slum, or else I go back home and babysit for my

33

sister's kids, with everybody laughing at me for being such a fool."

Anastasia nodded. "Me, too," she said glumly. "I don't have a sister, so I wouldn't have to babysit for a sister's kids. But everybody would probably laugh at me, too, if I go back home."

"You got your hunnert and nineteen dollars?" the girl asked.

"Yeah." Anastasia patted her pocketbook, where in a zippered compartment she was carrying the cash for the modeling course. "It's my life's savings."

"Mine, too. I earned it last summer, babysitting." The black girl stared at the hideous staircase. "Wonder how far we could get on a bus, with all that money. You wanta go over to the Trailways station and see? Maybe we could have us a weekend in Atlantic City or something."

"I don't think so," Anastasia said. "My parents are expecting me home for dinner."

"Mine, too. I was only kidding. What's your name?"

"Anastasia."

"That's cool. Mine's Henry."

"*Henry?*"

"Short for Henrietta. But if you call me that, you die."

"Oh. Okay." Anastasia laughed nervously.

"Only kidding," Henry said. "Hey, I'm going up. You coming?"

"Yes," Anastasia said decisively. "If you will, I will."

Together, they started up the stairs to Studio Charmante. In her mind, Anastasia began to revise the opening paragraphs of her school project.

My Chosen Career

Sometimes, in preparing for your chosen career, you have to do some scary stuff. Like, if you want to be a doctor, you have to look at dead bodies.

And if you want to be a lawyer, sometimes you have to go to a prison and talk to ax murderers.

To be a bookstore owner, and to develop poise and self-confidence, maybe you might have to go up a dark staircase where there is a dead cigar maybe smoked by a criminal, lying on the third step.

But you have to be brave as you set out on your chosen career.

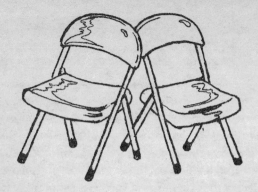

4

Soft lighting? Wrong. It was bare bulbs with pull chains hanging from the ceiling.

Thick beige carpeting? Wrong. It was dirty linoleum, green and white rectangles, with a mashed cigarette butt in one corner.

Long couches with bright cushions? Wrong. Three plastic chairs.

Glamorous receptionist at a curved desk with a bank of telephones? Wrong. It was a metal desk with an ancient typewriter, and an overweight woman talking loudly on the single black phone.

"So I told him this joke," she was saying, "about the two Europeans who went hunting and got eaten by bears, and when the forest rangers killed the bears, they said, 'The Czech's in the male?' But he didn't think it was funny. So I said, 'Well, the check *is* in the mail. I mailed it myself two days ago,' but he — listen, Selma, I gotta hang up. Someone's here. I'll call you back, okay?"

She put the telephone down, turned to the girls, and smiled. There was lipstick on her front teeth.

"Krupnik and Peabody, right?" she asked, looking down at a piece of paper.

Anastasia nodded. So did Henry. The woman checked off their names on the paper.

"Which one's which?" she asked, looking up.

"I'm Anastasia Krupnik," Anastasia told her.

"Then you must be Henrietta Peabo —"

"Call me that and you die. It's Henry Peabody."

Anastasia cringed. She couldn't imagine saying that to anyone, even someone whose front teeth were streaked with lipstick. But the woman laughed. "Gotcha," she said. "Okay, kids, welcome. I'm Aunt Vera. Now first we have some finances to take care of here."

Henry spoke up. "Hold it," she said. "What's with the Aunt Vera? I don't need any extra relatives. I got all the aunts I want already."

The woman chuckled. "You're feisty, Peabody. I like that. Tell you what. If you'd rather call me by my full name you can. It's Mrs. Szcempelowski."

Henry scowled.

"Everybody calls me Aunt Vera. It's easier. It doesn't mean you have to send flowers on my birthday or anything."

"Well, okay then," Henry said. "I was just checking."

"The other kids are inside with Uncle Charley — that's Mr. Szcempelowski, if you prefer — except for one who hasn't shown up yet. So let's get the finances taken care of, and you can go on in. I need a hundred nineteen dollars from each of you."

Henry and Anastasia looked at each other. Anastasia

37

was thinking of the alternatives. There didn't seem to be many. Her other choice was to go home and feel sorry for herself for a week. Henry's, she knew, was to babysit with her sister's children.

They each handed over their money to Aunt Vera, who counted it carefully and wrote out two receipts.

"Okay," she said, "you go on in through that door. I'll wait out here till the last one arrives and then I'll join you. Hey," she added, looking at their glum faces, "brighten up, will you? This is going to be *fun!*"

As Anastasia followed Henry through the door, she could hear Aunt Vera dial the telephone. "Selma?" Aunt Vera said. "So anyway, like I was saying, I told him I'd mailed the check, and he said . . ."

The room was brightly lighted, but Anastasia could see that it was lighted with fluorescent lights. She hated fluorescent lights. They made you look so ugly. Even if you didn't have a single flaw in your face, fluorescent lights created them. Her mother agreed. Mrs. Krupník said that fluorescent lights made your face look wrinkled and *old*. When they had moved the summer before into the big old house where they now lived, electricians had come and changed the lights in the bathrooms because Mrs. Krupnik said she would fall into a depression if she had to look at herself every day in a mirror with fluorescent lights above it.

At least, Anastasia thought, peering into the room, there were no mirrors.

As a matter of fact, there was not much of *anything*.

Just a brightly lighted room with the same green and white linoleum on the floor and a few metal folding chairs. Two girls about her own age were sitting there staring at their laps. A huge bald man was fooling with some video equipment in the back of the room.

"Come on in!" he called in a booming voice. "I'm Uncle Charley! Find yourselves a seat and introduce yourselves. Let's all be friends here! By the end of the week we'll be bosom buddies, right?"

"No way," muttered Henry. "Sit by me, Anastasia, okay?"

Anastasia followed Henry into the room and they sat down beside each other, far away from the other two girls. One didn't look up. The other, a plump redhead, glanced over with a hostile look. Anastasia smiled nervously at her; Henry glared.

"Watch out for that one," Henry whispered to Anastasia. "That one's evil."

Uncle Charley puttered some more with the video camera that stood on a big tripod. "Damn rental equipment — it never works right," he said. Finally he announced, "There. I think I got it." He came to the front of the room, grinning. "Welcome, ladies. We got one more coming and then we'll get started. A few introductory words from me and Aunt Vera, and then we're going to have us some fun with the camera. You'll all be TV stars, how about that?"

The redheaded girl said in a bored voice, "I've already been on real TV. I was on *Community Auditions* last year."

Anastasia could hear Henry, beside her, give a low groan.

"Well, that's real nice, honey," Uncle Charley boomed. "It'll be real helpful to have someone with so much experience in the class." He walked to the doorway and called, "Vera? That last one show up yet?"

Aunt Vera answered something, and Uncle Charley called back, "Good. Bring him on in so we can get started!"

Him? Anastasia looked at Henry in surprise. A *boy?* Henry rolled her eyes.

Aunt Vera appeared in the doorway, smiling with her lipsticky teeth showing. "Find a seat, son," she said, and stood aside to let a short, stocky boy through. Anastasia didn't want to stare, so she glanced over quickly. She saw a pair of blue trousers. A white shirt and necktie. *Necktie?* That was weird. She and Henry and the other two girls were all dressed casually in jeans. She glanced again at the boy. He had something in his hand. A leather briefcase. *Briefcase?* The only boy she had ever known who carried a briefcase was—

The boy looked at Anastasia and his face lit up. "Anastasia Krupnik!" he said.

Oh, no. Oh, *no!* It couldn't be. But it was.

It was Robert Giannini.

Anastasia had known Robert Giannini since they were both five years old. They had gone to kindergarten together, and every grade through sixth, until her family had moved away from Cambridge the summer before.

He had been a wimp even when he was five, even though he didn't have his briefcase then. He had had a little plaid bookbag in kindergarten, filled with pencils that had his name printed on them.

He had always brought nutritious lunches to school, little salads in plastic containers and vitamin pills. He had brought nose drops — *nose drops!* — to school because he had allergies, and three times a day, for seven years, Anastasia had had to watch Robert Giannini sit at his desk, throw his head back, and stick a medicine dropper in each nostril. Talk about gross.

He had always offered to be Monitor. Crayon Monitor, Paper Monitor, Hall Monitor: anything that needed a monitor, Robert Giannini had always volunteered. In fourth grade, in a science book, there had been a picture of a monitor lizard, and after that everyone had called Robert Giannini "Monitor Lizard" behind his back.

In fourth grade he got his briefcase, which he had carried ever since. Each year he had become more and more of a wimp until, in sixth grade, he was a world-class wimp, no question.

He wore orthopedic shoes.

He wore galoshes when it rained.

He watched Channel 2, the educational channel, every single night, and then gave oral reports in class on the programs he had seen, for extra credit. Once — Anastasia could hardly bear even to think about this — he had given a report on human reproduction. Right in front of the entire sixth-grade class, Robert Giannini had stood up and talked about human reproduction, actually

41

saying the words "sperm" and "ova" *out loud*. It was the most embarrassing thing that ever happened in sixth grade.

But since she had started seventh grade, junior high, in a whole different town, Anastasia had assumed that she would never see him again. She had *vowed* she would never see him again.

Yet here he was, clutching his leather briefcase, shoving aside a chair so that he could — she looked up — yes; he was actually about to sit down next to her.

Anastasia had spent her entire age-thirteen life, four months so far, trying to forget that she had ever known a jerk like Robert Giannini.

And now Robert Giannini had enrolled in modeling school.

"Now that we're all here, let's introduce ourselves," Uncle Charley announced in his booming voice from the front of the room. "You already know me and Aunt Vera. And you'll be hearing a lot from us this week. So let's hear a little from you. Your name, a little about yourself, and what you hope to get out of the course. Okay? We'll start with you, honey, right here in the front."

The dark-haired girl who had been staring at her lap jumped. She looked up nervously. "Me?" she whispered.

"Yep. Tell us your name. I have it written on my list, of course, but the other kids don't know you yet."

The girl whispered something. Anastasia couldn't hear what she said.

"Sweetie," Aunt Vera said, "try speaking up a little louder."

"Helen Margaret Howell," the girl said, blushing.

"Good. How old are you, Helen?" asked Aunt Vera.

"Helen Margaret," the girl whispered.

"Oh. Well, Helen Margaret, how old are you?"

"Twelve," Helen Margaret whispered.

"And what would you like to tell us about yourself?"

Helen Margaret shook her head. "I don't know."

"Well," Aunt Vera said, "what interesting things have happened in your life lately?"

Helen Margaret said nothing. She stared at the floor.

Aunt Vera nodded cheerfully. "You're a little nervous, honey. You'll get over that. Next? You?" She pointed to the redheaded girl.

"My name's Bambi, like the deer, but it's spelled with an "e" — Bambie," the girl said in a loud voice. "Bambie Browne — the Browne has an 'e' too. I'm fourteen, and I'm planning a career in the entertainment field. I was on *Community Auditions* last year. I did a monologue. And I do a lot of beauty pageants. My coach said I ought to take this course to pick up some pointers. I won Miss Cranberry Bog when I was ten. My dress was made-to-order and it was the only one in the contest that wasn't cranberry-colored. I had green, see, because of my hair. My hair color's natural. And — "

"Thank you. Next?" Aunt Vera looked toward Henry.

"My name's Henry Peabody and I'm thirteen and I came because I wanted to learn something about maybe being a model. My aunt — that's my real aunt, not no fake aunt — said maybe I could be a model because I'm tall and thin. And if I could be a model I could earn enough money to go to college." She paused. Then she added, "My hair color's natural, too. So's my skin." She grinned.

Anastasia squirmed in her chair. She knew it was her turn next and she didn't know what to say. Aunt Vera smiled at her.

"Well, ah, my name's Anastasia Krupnik. I'm thirteen, same as Henry. And I'm tall and thin, too, same as Henry, but I guess I wasn't really thinking about actually being a model. I think I'm going to be a bookstore owner. I was just sort of hoping to, I don't know, maybe get more self-confidence."

"Good. Bobby?"

Robert Giannini stood up. *Typical*, Anastasia thought. Nobody else stood up, but Robert Giannini stood up. "That's Robert," he said, "not Bobby. I've never been called Bobby. I'm thirteen but I haven't achieved my full growth yet so I appear younger. I'm expecting a growth spurt anytime."

Anastasia put her head in her hands. *Growth spurt.* What a Robert Giannini–like thing to say.

"I enrolled," Robert went on, "just out of general interest. I haven't chosen a career yet. I'm considering metallurgy. I don't think of myself as a potential entertainer or anything, although there are several magic tricks that I do quite well. But I like to explore all kinds of possibilities. If I find that I photograph well, then of course television would be one of my options — "

Anastasia could tell that he was going to go on and on. Apparently Uncle Charley could tell that, too, because he interrupted Robert.

"Good," said Uncle Charley. "Now that we know each other, let's get started."

"You wanta go to McDonald's for lunch?" asked Henry. "Or do you want to just walk over to the park and throw up?"

Anastasia giggled. They had just left Studio Charmante for their lunch break and were standing together on the windy street corner. Back at the studio, Robert Giannini had cornered Uncle Charley to discuss camera angles. Bambie Browne had disappeared someplace, probably to the ladies' room to repair her mascara, and Helen Margaret was sitting all alone in the waiting room, opening a paper bag of sandwiches that she had brought with her.

"I can't," Anastasia told Henry apologetically. "I have to meet someone for lunch. I'm sorry."

Henry's eyes lit up. "Some guy?"

"No, nobody interesting. A woman. But I'll see you back here at one o'clock, okay?"

"Okay. I'm going to get me a Big Mac and then I want to hang out at the record store. Maybe I'll listen to a little Shakespeare for this afternoon," Henry said, laughing. "I'll practice a few gestures."

Anastasia laughed too, said goodbye, and headed off in the opposite direction.

It had been a weird morning. So far, Uncle Charley had videotaped three of the kids — all but Henry and Anastasia; he would do them after lunch.

"Now, try to be natural," he had said. "This is just for the 'Before' part. At the end of the week, we'll do the 'After,' and you'll see what a difference has taken place. Let's start with you, Helen Margaret. I want you to stand up here in front and simply talk about yourself a little. Look toward the camera."

Helen Margaret walked to the front of the room as if she were made of wood. She stood in the place Uncle Charley indicated, looked at the floor, and was silent.

"Okay, sweetie," Aunt Vera said, "the camera's rolling. Tell us about yourself. Look up. We won't bite."

Helen Margaret, with her head still down, peered up through her straggly dark bangs. "I don't know what to say," she mumbled.

"You got any hobbies?" Uncle Charley called from behind the camera.

Helen Margaret bit her lip and shook her head. "No," she whispered.

"How about a boyfriend?" asked Aunt Vera.

"No."

Anastasia wanted to point out to Aunt Vera that she wasn't asking open-ended questions. But she decided that maybe it was a little early in the course to start correcting the head person. So she kept quiet.

The interview — or lack of interview — went on for ten minutes, with Helen Margaret mumbling one-word answers to questions while she looked at the floor.

Anastasia felt sorry for her. I'm not going to *like* it when it's my turn, she thought, but at least I can stand up straight and say something. I can tell about my family and stuff.

Bambie went next. She posed in the front of the room and began her performance before Uncle Charley got the camera started. "Hold it," he called. "Start again."

Bambie tossed her head, smoothed her hair, and waited until the camera was on. "I'm doing the monologue that I did for *Community Auditions*," she announced. "This is Juliet's death scene."

Next to Anastasia, Henry groaned quietly. Anastasia squirmed in embarrassment as Bambie gestured with her hands, holding up an imaginary vial of poison. " 'Shall I not then be stifled in the vault, to whose foul mouth no healthsome air breathes in,' " she intoned dramatically, " 'and there die strangled ere my Romeo comes?' " She pretended to drink from the imaginary poison and began to sink to the floor. Mid-sink, she called to Uncle Charley, "Is the camera getting this? I don't have to go all the way to the floor. I could collapse across a chair. I practice it both ways."

Uncle Charley turned the camera off. "We got enough, sweetheart," he said.

"Robert?" Aunt Vera suggested. "How about you next?"

Robert Giannini picked up his briefcase and carried it to the front of the room. I wonder what he *keeps* in that briefcase, Anastasia thought.

I wonder what he's going to *say*.

47

If he makes his speech on Human Reproduction, I'm leaving. I'll forfeit my whole $119 if I have to, but I will never again in my life sit still and listen to Robert Giannini say, "Out of ten million sperm, only one will reach the ovum."

Robert cleared his throat, adjusted his tie, and began, "I am going to speak about the United States Space Program."

"Zzzzzzzzz." Henry faked a snore.

Anastasia sighed, remembering the morning, as she headed across the Boston Common toward Beacon Hill. Modeling school wasn't really what she had anticipated. Henry Peabody was the only good thing about it.

Walking, she tried to think of some open-ended questions for the bookstore owner. But her mind kept wandering instead, revising her paper on My Chosen Career.

Anastasia Krupnik

My Chosen Career

Sometimes, in doing the necessary preparation for your chosen career, you will encounter people that you wish you hadn't encountered.

Maybe they will be people from your past — people you hoped you would never see again under any circumstances ever.

Sometimes they may be people you have never met before, the kind of people who recite Shakespeare with gestures and then do a disgusting curtsy at the end.

I think there is probably no way to avoid this happening. Moving to an entirely new town doesn't seem to be the solution.

Maybe moving to another country would help.

5

Anastasia made her way through the Common, averting her eyes from the wino who sat slumped on a bench, slurping booze out of a bottle concealed in a paper bag. She stopped briefly to pat a tall, thin dog who came to her with a stick in his mouth and his tail wagging furiously, until the dog's master called, "Come, Sheba," and the dog reluctantly but obediently trotted away.

She walked around the State House with its glistening golden dome and found the street she was looking for. Here, on Beacon Hill, it was quieter, less crowded. The streets were narrow, lined with brick sidewalks, trees, and gaslights. There didn't seem to be any stores here, just tall brick houses close to each other.

Her father had told her that once, in the last century, these were all private homes. Now, though, most of them had been divided into apartments. Only a few people still owned entire houses on Beacon Hill. *Rich* people.

Anastasia checked the numbers and began walking downhill. She had a horrible thought. What if the bookstore, Pages, was actually in someone's home? A *rich* person's home? What if the bookstore owner, Ms. Barbara Page, was old, rich, and grouchy?

She looked down at her legs and feet. Her hiking boots were coated with gray slush and the bottoms of her jeans were soggy. *Great.* She had a sudden, horrible vision of an old, rich, grouchy bookstore owner staring at her with hatred as she stood dripping on the polished floor of the bookstore.

She pictured a newspaper headline that said: JUNIOR HIGH STUDENT THROTTLED TO DEATH BY ENRAGED BEACON HILL BOOKSTORE OWNER.

She pictured a smaller headline underneath: "SHE GOT SLUSH ON MY RARE VOLUMES," EXPLAINS BARBARA PAGE.

And finally, Anastasia pictured a third, smaller, sadder newspaper caption: Justifiable homicide, says judge.

"Grab that leg!" a man's voice yelled suddenly, and Anastasia jumped. She backed away from the voice. Which leg did he mean to grab — her right or her left? Could she kick with the other?

Then she realized that the voice had come from the back of a truck which had the title GREAT MOVES painted on the side. Two men were wrestling with a heavy green sofa. She remembered when her own family had moved from Cambridge, and that the moving men had wrestled the same way with their furniture. They had yelled, too. Actually, they had yelled things a lot worse than "Grab that leg," she remembered.

She paused and waited until the men, grunting, carried the sofa across the sidewalk and up the front steps of a house. Then she walked on and suddenly she was there.

51

Whew. It wasn't a whole house. It was a real store, a real bookstore, in the basement of an old brick building. A carved wooden sign that said PAGES was in the window.

Relieved, Anastasia took off her glove and pushed open the door. A bell attached to the top of the door tinkled, signaling her entrance.

"Hi. I'm Barbara Page, and you must be Anastasia Krupnik. Why don't you take off your boots?" the bookstore owner said. "Your feet must be freezing."

Anastasia said hi, knelt, and began to unlace her boots. Her feet *were* freezing, she realized. Then she realized something else. Something embarrassing. She looked up. "This is embarrassing," she said, "but the socks I have on . . ."

Barbara Page looked, and laughed. "One's blue and the other's brown. That's okay. Leave your boots there in the corner and come on into the back room with me. I have some sandwiches there for us."

Anastasia followed the woman, looking around at the cluttered, colorful store. Bookstores were among Anastasia's favorite places; maybe they were even first on her list, or at least tied for first with libraries. She sometimes thought that she would like to live in a library, not even having a kitchen — just going out to eat, and spending all the rest of her life surrounded by books.

But maybe it would be even better to live in a bookstore. Heck, if you owned the bookstore you could even put a kitchen in the back — she could see now, entering the back room, that Barbara Page did have a coffeepot there, and a small sink — and you'd never have to leave at all. Just live surrounded by walls of bookshelves. Read and read and read, and sometimes stop to eat a little. What a great life.

Suddenly Anastasia began to feel very happy about her chosen career.

"Do you *live* here?" she asked.

Barbara Page nodded. "Sort of," she said. "Actually, my husband and I live upstairs, in the house part. But I just come down that little staircase over there every morning —" she pointed, and Anastasia could see the bottom of a narrow staircase behind a partly opened door — "and voilà! I'm at work."

"That's neat."

Barbara Page uncovered some sandwiches that were waiting on a paper plate. She poured Coke into two plastic glasses.

"You're right," she said. "It *is* neat. Hey, how's your dad? I love your dad's books. Is he working on a new one?"

Anastasia nodded. "Yeah, but it won't be done for a long time. He's right at the point where he says he's going to burn the whole thing up and start a new career, maybe as a tennis pro."

"I didn't know he played tennis."

"He doesn't. But it doesn't matter, because he's not *really* going to be a tennis pro. It's just what he says when he's in the middle of a new book. After he says that, it's usually about six months before the book is done."

"Here. Eat." Barbara Page handed Anastasia half of a tuna fish sandwich, and Anastasia took a bite.

The telephone on the messy desk rang. The bookstore owner swallowed her own bite of sandwich, picked up the phone, and said, "Pages, good afternoon."

Anastasia listened while she ate her sandwich and sipped at her Coke. It wasn't really eavesdropping, she figured, because after all, she was sitting right there beside the telephone. And anyway, it was a business call, so it was a good way to get information about her chosen career.

"Well, Mrs. Devereaux, I'm really sorry to hear that," Barbara Page was saying. "It got great reviews, and I thought it was exactly the kind of book you'd like."

She listened for a moment, making a silent face at Anastasia, and then went on, "I wouldn't call it trashy, Mrs. Devereaux. The *New York Times* said it was hard-hitting and realistic, but they thought it was brilliant. And the author *did* win the Pulitzer Prize last year."

Finally, after listening again, she said politely, "Of *course* you can return it. I'll just credit your account. You drop it off next time you're down this way."

After she had hung up, she groaned. "That woman. Honestly. She buys books, reads them, and then returns them and asks for her money back. You'd think she'd go to the library instead.

"This is the third one she's returned since September.

And she always spills coffee on them, too, so I can't resell them."

Anastasia was astonished. "But that's not *fair!*" she said.

Barbara Page chuckled. "It's the breaks," she said.

While Anastasia ate her sandwich and drank her Coke, she listened to Barbara Page answer the telephone three more times. She listened to her say to someone, "I don't carry cassettes, I'm afraid. But you could try Barnes and Noble."

Then she heard her say to someone else, "I do *have* that book here, Mr. Phelps. But to be honest, I don't think it would be the right birthday gift for your mother. She's had trouble reading since her cataract surgery. I think maybe a record album would be a better choice, at least until her eyes are stronger. I know she loves Bach. Why don't you get her a recording of *The Magnificat?*"

And finally, to the third caller, she said, "Gosh, that's been out of print for years. But I bet anything you could find it at the library, Mrs. MacDonald. Or if you want to *own* it, you could try a secondhand bookstore."

After the last phone call, Anastasia said, "I don't mean to be rude or anything, but how do you make any money? I mean, my dad said that you gave forty-seven people wine and cheese and only sold three books, and now you tell me that you let people return books with coffee spilled on them, and you tell them to buy records, and you send them to other bookstores, and I don't see how — "

Suddenly Anastasia looked around, through the door into the bookstore itself. It looked exactly the way a bookstore *should*, in Anastasia's opinion, look: walled with ceiling-high bookcases, vivid with the colorful jackets of novels, and in one corner she could see a child-size table and chairs beside the shelves that held children's books. A lavishly illustrated book lay on the bright yellow table, open to a page that showed rabbits in jogging shoes running along a country road.

But something was missing.

While Barbara Page watched, Anastasia adjusted her glasses, frowned, and peered through the door, trying to figure out what was missing.

Finally she turned back to the bookstore owner. "There aren't any customers," she said, puzzled.

Barbara Page shrugged, smiling. "Sometimes there are," she said. "Never very many, though, I'm afraid."

"But how do you make a living? How do you pay the rent?" Anastasia asked.

A man's voice interrupted their conversation. "Barb?" he called down the back stairs.

"What, honey?" the bookstore owner called back.

"Where's yesterday's *Wall Street Journal*?" the man called.

"On your desk. You left it there last night," Barbara Page replied. Then she turned back to Anastasia with a sheepish grin. "*That's* how I pay the rent. There isn't any rent. We own the whole building — my husband and I."

"Oh."

"You look disappointed."

"No," Anastasia said, "not disappointed. Just confused.

56

I mean, I'm glad you have a husband — he sounded like a nice guy — and I know lots of professional women have husbands. My mother does, for example."

"Why are you confused, then?"

"Well, what if when I grow up and start my chosen career, I don't have a husband who owns a building that I can put my chosen career in?"

"Then," Barbara Page said decisively, "you work hard and become successful and you buy your own building. I bet you could buy two or three buildings eventually, Anastasia. You look like a hard worker. Here — have some potato chips."

Anastasia took one and munched. She thought about it. It was true that she was a hard worker. She probably *would* be a successful bookstore owner. Heck, she could probably end up owning skyscrapers.

But it might *help*, she realized, to marry someone who *also* owned buildings.

"You know what?" she said to Barbara Page. "I think I have to leave my options open."

"What do you mean, exactly?"

"Well, I want to be an independent person and all that, and a hard worker, and a successful bookstore owner who buys skyscrapers, but — "

"But what?"

"But if I happen to fall in love with a very rich man along the way, I want to be prepared. I want to have poise and self-confidence and good posture and a sense of fashion, because a rich husband-to-be probably wouldn't get real turned on by these blue jeans and these dumb socks that don't match, right? But I'm already taking a course — I didn't tell you about this yet, but I'm taking a course in — oh, good grief, what time is it?" Anastasia pushed the sleeve of her sweat shirt back and looked at her watch. "It's almost one o'clock already! I have to go! Rats!"

"Hey, this was fun, Anastasia. I'm glad your dad sent you over. It gets lonely in here sometimes. I'm sorry you can't stay longer."

"But . . ." Anastasia looked at Barbara Page in dismay. "But what?"

"I forgot to do the interview!" Anastasia wailed.

"So come back."

"Can I? I mean *may* I?"

"Sure. Not tomorrow, because every Tuesday I have a senior citizens group in here for lunch and a book talk, and let's see, Thursday's no good because every Thursday I have the local nursery school kids come in for a story hour — "

"Do they buy books? Do any of them buy books?"

Barbara Page laughed. "Occasionally. And they do *love* books; that's what matters. Come Wednesday, okay?"

"Okay. I'll come. And I'll do the interview for sure. And more than that — "

"More than that what?"

"I'll buy a book," Anastasia told her. "I really will. And in the meantime, I'll give a lot more thought to my project."

My Chosen Career

Even if you are a good-natured person who loves your chosen career, and even if you happen to have a husband and together you own the building that your chosen career is in, still it is important to be a hard-nosed businessperson sometimes.

You cannot allow people to spill coffee on your stuff.

6

"You look tired," Mrs. Krupnik said as Anastasia came through the back door and flopped into a kitchen chair without removing her jacket.

"I am," Anastasia said, "I'm totaled. Hi, Dad. What on earth are you doing?"

Her father was at the kitchen table with a stack of magazines and a pair of scissors. He made a wry face. "I'm doing Sam's nursery school homework assignment. Why in the world do they tell a three-year-old kid to cut out pictures of trucks when he hasn't even mastered the use of scissors?" Dr. Krupnik turned a page, frowned at a picture of a moving van, and picked up the scissors. "How was your day? I hope they didn't give *you* any assignments that you can't handle."

"My day was wei — " Anastasia stopped. She remembered how much her father hated the word "weird." "It was odd," she said. "No, I don't have homework. I'm just supposed to practice poise. I'm supposed to speak distinctly and look people in the eye when I talk to them."

Her father, furrowing his eyebrows, was carefully cutting around the tires of the moving van. "Don't look me in the eye when I'm doing this," he said, "or I'll wreck it."

"Don't look me in the eye while I'm beating these egg whites," her mother said, "or I'll let the mixer run too long and ruin the meringue." She turned on the electric mixer.

Anastasia shrugged and began to take off her jacket. "Great," she said. "Where's Sam? I'll look Sam in the eye."

"Here I am," called Sam from someplace invisible. "Under the table."

"What are you doing under the table?" Anastasia asked. She picked up the corner of the tablecloth, peered in, and saw her brother huddled there.

"Playing cave man," Sam said happily.

Anastasia knelt and put her head under the tablecloth. "Look me in the eye, Sam," she commanded.

Sam stared at his sister.

Anastasia stared back at him. She looked him in the eye and spoke distinctly. "Cave man is a dumb game," she said. "It's boring to sit under a table."

"Yeah, I know," Sam said. "I'm quitting now." He crawled out from his cave.

"You now what else is boring?" Dr. Krupnik said, putting the scissors down and stroking his beard. "Cutting out trucks. Is this enough, Sam? I did eight."

Sam looked at the truck pictures. "Okay," he said.

"Good," said his father. "Anastasia, look me in the eye, please, and practice poise."

Anastasia looked her father in the eye. She straightened her shoulders.

"Good," he said. "Now, I would love it if you would go to the refrigerator and get me out a nice cold beer. Then I want you to tell me about your day."

"Coming right up," Anastasia said distinctly.

"Well, one good thing," Anastasia said after her father had opened his beer and had a sip. "I made a new friend. A girl, but her name is Henry. It's really Henrietta, but if you call her that you die."

"I once knew a girl with a boy's name: Stevie," her mother said. She had spread the meringue over a lemon pie and was putting it into the oven. "I think her real name was probably Stephanie, but she liked to be called Stevie."

"I know a girl named Nicky at nursery school," said Sam, "but I hate her."

"Don't say 'hate,' sweetie," Mrs. Krupnik told him. "It's okay to say that you don't care much for her, but 'hate' isn't a nice word."

Sam scowled. "I know a girl named Nicky at nursery school," he repeated, "and I don't care for her so much that I would like to run over her with a very big truck."

Mrs. Krupnik adjusted the temperature of the oven. "Well," she said, "that's a slightly better way of putting it, I guess."

"Go on, Anastasia," said her father. "More about your day."

Anastasia told them about Bambie and her monologue from *Romeo and Juliet*. Her parents laughed and laughed.

"We always watch *Bambi* on the VCR at my school," Sam went on. "*Bambi* is my very favorite VCR thing, except maybe *Dumbo*."

"Bambie with an 'e,'" Anastasia reminded him. "Not the deer Bambi."

"Do you hate her?" Sam asked. "I mean, do you not care for her very much?"

Anastasia frowned. "I guess that's right. I don't care very much for Bambie."

Then she told them about Helen Margaret.

"Do you not care for her very much?" Sam asked.

"She's okay," Anastasia said. "I guess I'm worried about her. I think she's going to flunk poise. She can't do the looking-people-in-the-eye part. It's not easy to look people in the eye. But if you force yourself, you should be able to do it."

"I can do it easy," Sam said. "Watch me." He came to stand beside Anastasia's chair and leaned forward until his forehead touched hers. He stared at her without blinking for a long moment. "See? I can do it."

"Right," Anastasia told him. "But Helen Margaret can't. She tries, but then she always looks away, down at the floor."

"It sounds as if she's terribly shy," Mrs. Krupnik said. "Maybe by the end of the week she'll relax a little."

"I hope so," Anastasia said. Then she told them about Robert Giannini.

"*Robert Giannini?*" Mrs. Krupnik said. "I can't believe that Robert Giannini actually enrolled in modeling school. He was such an odd little boy, though. I guess I shouldn't be surprised at anything he does."

"Do you not care for him very much?" Sam asked.

"You got it, Sam," Anastasia said, laughing. "I don't care for Robert Giannini so much that I wish his dumb growth spurt would work in reverse and make him grow smaller and smaller until he disappears."

"I remember, Anastasia," said her mother, "that there was a time — it was when you were in sixth grade — that you kind of *liked* Robert Giannini. He was sort of your boyfriend."

Anastasia groaned. "*Mom,*" she said, "I was young then. And completely without poise."

"Well," Anastasia's father said, "the whole modeling course experience is interesting, but I'd like to hear about your interview with Barbara Page."

"Can we eat first? I'm starving. And also, it's complicated. Barbara Page is a terrific person, Dad. She's probably one of the *nicest* people I've ever met. She's . . . well, what would you call someone who loves everybody and wants to make everybody happy and doesn't mind giving stuff away in order to do that?"

"Generous," suggested Mrs. Krupnik.

"Looney Tunes," suggested Dr. Krupnik.

"Nope," said Sam. "I know what you would call that person because we have a story at school about it. It's called 'The Person with the Heart of Gold.' "

Anastasia stared at Sam. She nodded. "That," she said, "is what Barbara Page should have named her bookstore."

"Tell me all about it. I want to know every detail. And also, what did your family have for dessert tonight?" Sonya Isaacson was on the telephone.

Anastasia giggled. "Lemon meringue pie. Sam is into imaginary skiing, so he asked Mom to make a dessert that looked like snow. She considered baked Alaska, but that's too complicated to make, and so she made lemon meringue pie instead. Why?"

Sonya sighed. "I'm going to Weight Loss Clinic this week. Great vacation, huh? Every day I have to stand on the scales, and I have to write down everything I eat, but that's no big deal, because I only get to eat teeny-weeny portions of everything, and you know what I had for dessert? Half an apple. Tell me *all* about it."

"Well, let's see, I took the bus in, and I got there at nine-fifteen, and — "

"No, wait. I didn't mean modeling school. Of course I want to know about modeling school. But I meant, first of all, tell me all about the lemon meringue pie, every single detail."

Anastasia, in her pajamas, sat on her bed and brushed her hair. "Frank," she said to her goldfish, "tomorrow is Hair Restyling Day at my modeling course."

Frank said "oh" silently.

65

"If you were part of the singles scene, Frank, instead of a loner, would you prefer a female with long or short hair?"

Frank stared at her.

"Curly, or straight?" Anastasia asked, dragging the brush through her hair.

He stared, and flipped his tail.

"Punk style, maybe? But I wouldn't want it dyed weird colors. I saw this girl once with her hair dyed *orange*. That was sooooo gross."

She looked at him, and he looked back at her mournfully. "I'm sorry, Frank," Anastasia said apologetically. "I forgot that you're orange. It really is an okay color for a goldfish."

Frank wiggled his behind happily.

"Also," Anastasia went on, "if you were a married goldfish, Frank, how would you feel about supporting your wife financially in her chosen career? My dad says that I would probably feel happier if I were independent and financially successful, and he said there's no reason why I couldn't be that way as a bookstore owner, and that maybe he sent me to the wrong bookstore owner for an interview, even though Barbara Page is a terrific lady —

"Frank? You're not listening to me!"

Frank formed a very large "Oooooh" with his mouth. If he could speak out loud, Anastasia thought, he would speak very distinctly. And he certainly did look you right in the eye. One thing about old Frank, for sure; he had *poise*.

Anastasia Krupnik

My Chosen Career

A rich husband is not a necessity for a bookstore owner.

But if you don't have a rich husband, it is probably not a good idea to have a Heart of Gold. It is necessary, according to one person I interviewed,* to have a Heart of Steel. You have to learn to say no to people who want to return books with coffee stains, and you have to sell books to people who have bad eyesight even if they would prefer records, and you can't serve lunch once a week to groups of senior citizens.

It is all right, though, to serve wine and cheese to forty-seven people who come to meet a moderately well known poet.

Myron Krupnik, Ph.D., moderately well known poet

7

"Don't even take your coats off, kids," Aunt Vera said to the five modeling-course students when they arrived at Studio Charmante on Tuesday morning. "For Hair Styling we go across the street."

"Across the street," Henry Peabody muttered to Anastasia, "is a Chinese restaurant. They think they're making won ton soup outta my hair, they better think again."

"I always put mousse on my hair," Bambie Browne announced loudly. "It gives body and highlights."

"Bullwinkle Moose?" Henry asked in an innocent voice, and Bambie glared.

Helen Margaret squinted through her shaggy bangs and didn't say anything.

"I'll stay here and man the phone," Uncle Charley

announced, and eased his enormous bulk into the chair at the front desk. During the entire day before, the phone had not rung once. But Anastasia could understand why Uncle Charley didn't want to participate in the hair styling. Uncle Charley had no hair. Not a single hair on his head.

Aunt Vera, holding a scruffy-looking fake-fur coat around her, led the way down the stairs. She guided the four girls, with Robert Giannini and his briefcase bringing up the rear, across the street, through a door beside the Chinese restaurant, up a flight of stairs, and into a beauty parlor.

It was not much different from Studio Charmante: the same fluorescent lights, the same crummy linoleum floor. But the walls were pink, and decorated with posters of hair styles. There was a row of sinks, each with its own vinyl beauty-parlor chair, and a row of hair dryers.

And there were three old ladies wearing pink smocks. They looked like triplets: gray-haired triplets.

Once, Anastasia remembered, she had read that there was a special place where all old elephants went to die. Elephants walked for hundreds of miles, across the plains of Africa, when they were old, in order to die in this special secret place.

It had never occurred to her before that there might also be a special secret place, upstairs over a Chinese restaurant in Boston, for ancient beauticians. She pictured them in distant cities — Cleveland and Phoenix and Boise — realizing that the time had come, packing up their plastic curlers and their styling brushes, and starting across the country on their long, final journey to the place where beauticians went to die.

Nervously Anastasia's hand went to her knitted cap. She was almost afraid to take it off.

"Okay," Aunt Vera said cheerfully. "Hang your coats up. Helen Margaret, Bambie, and Robert — we'll have them do you first. Henry and Anastasia? You can sit down over there while you wait."

Anastasia noticed with some satisfaction that Robert and Bambie both looked just as nervous as she was. Helen Margaret, of course, looked nervous all the time, so her look hadn't changed.

She watched Robert sit down apprehensively in one of the pink vinyl chairs. His briefcase was in his lap, and one of the old ladies covered it — and most of Robert — with a plastic cloth which she tied behind his neck like a bib. She removed his glasses and set them carefully on the counter.

"I suppose you'll want to shape my sideburns," Robert said in a loud, panicky voice, "but you'll find that my sideburns are not very well formed yet because my facial hair is still somewhat sparse and — "

He was cut off in midsentence because the old lady, with a surprising show of manual dexterity, had released a lever that tilted the chair backward. Robert suddenly went from vertical to horizontal; his feet, in their old-man lace-up leather shoes, shot out straight, and his head disappeared backward into the sink. The old lady

70

turned on the water and began to shoot him with a rubber hose.

"Lookit that," announced Henry Peabody. "She drowned him. Him and his facial hair both."

Helen Margaret had met a similar fate silently; she too was horizontal, under a hose.

Bambie, however, was resisting her fate with a monologue and gestures. "Wait, please," Bambie was announcing. "I want to be certain that you realize my hair *color* is natural — this red" (she gestured with a wave of her hand to indicate her head) "has come down through generations of my family. But the curls are created with special rollers that I sent away for, from a place in Calif—"

Then Bambie, still talking, was tilted backward, and her specially created curls disappeared into the sink.

Anastasia and Henry watched as Aunt Vera strolled around, peering into the sinks where Robert and Bambie were having their hair washed. Then she went to stand beside the old lady who was doing Helen Margaret.

"This is one with real potential," Anastasia heard Aunt Vera say in a low voice to the old lady who was rubbing shampoo into Helen Margaret's hair. "I want to supervise this one when you start the cut."

"Real potential?" murmured Henry in a low, surprised voice. "Potential for what? Miss Nervous America?"

"Shhhhh," Anastasia said, giggling. She poked Henry. "Look. Watch Robert."

Robert Giannini had been tilted upright again, and a

towel had been wrapped around his head like a turban. Without his glasses, wearing a turban, Robert had been transformed. He looked . . . well, thought Anastasia, he looked almost romantic. She remembered an old movie, *Lawrence of Arabia,* starring Peter O'Toole. Robert looked like that: Giannini of Arabia.

But after she rubbed his head briskly, the old lady whipped off the towel turban and handed Robert his glasses. He put them on and looked around. His damp hair stood up in spikes. He didn't look romantic at all. He just looked Giannini-esque, only worse.

Also, Anastasia realized, it was embarrassing to see a boy with his hair wet. At a swimming pool, okay. You *expected* it at a swimming pool. But in a room with pink walls, it was weird and embarrassing, as if he had just gotten out of the shower or something. She looked away as the old lady led Robert to a different chair.

Henry had picked up an old issue of *Vogue* and was leafing through it. "Look," she said, and pointed to a picture of a tall, elegant black woman wearing a yellow chiffon evening gown. "You think I could ever be a model like that?"

Anastasia examined the picture. Then she studied Henry Peabody. Henry's hair looked like the plastic Chore Girl her mother used to scrub pots and pans, and she had skewered it into place with green barrettes shaped like butterflies. She was wearing an oversize sweat shirt, jeans, and grubby sneakers. But she had a slender face, huge eyes, and a beautiful smile. And she was very tall — taller than Anastasia, who was five foot seven.

"Yes," Anastasia said. "I think you could."

"What if I went home tonight looking like that?" Henry said, laughing. "My mother would have a heart attack. Boy, if I go home looking like that, you might as well start dialing 911 for the ambulance to cart my mother away."

"Where do you live?"

"Dorchester. Just takes me about twenty minutes to get here on the T."

The T was Boston's subway. Anastasia nodded. "I come by bus," she said. "Robert comes on the T, though. He lives in Cambridge. I used to live near him."

She glanced over at Robert and blinked. "Hey, look," she said to Henry.

Robert was still bibbed in the plastic sheet, but he looked different. His mop of curly hair had been shaped into something sleeker, more sophisticated. He was staring at himself in the mirror while the old lady zapped the back of his neck with an electric razor.

Next to him, Bambie was chattering to the woman cutting her hair. "I should've brought my mousse," Bambie said. "Do you have mousse? I really need it for body and highlights."

"Hold your head still," the woman commanded, "or you'll get the point of these scissors right in your jugular."

Beside the third chair, Aunt Vera was watching intently as the third old lady snipped at Helen Margaret's dark hair. "The ears are exquisite," Aunt Vera said. "I want you to shape it carefully to expose those ears."

Exquisite ears? Anastasia had never in her life considered the possibility of ears being exquisite. Ears were *necessary*, period. You couldn't *hear* without ears. But she had never thought they were worth looking at.

Yet, watching, she could see that Helen Margaret did have small, perfectly shaped ears. Earlier they had been concealed by the thicket of dark hair that had also covered her forehead and most of her face.

Now her long, straggly bangs were gone. In their place was a smooth, even edge of hair above her eyebrows. The rest of her wet hair was combed sleekly back while the woman snipped carefully with her shiny scissors. Anastasia could see Helen Margaret's face for the first time. She could see the pale, almost translucent skin and a pair of deep blue, long-lashed eyes peering shyly into the mirror as the woman worked.

Helen Magaret was beautiful. Anastasia realized it with astonishment, and then she poked Henry and said it to her in a whisper. "Helen Margaret's beautiful."

Henry looked up from the magazine, where she was still studying the black woman in the yellow dress.

Henry stared. "Holy —" she began, and then fell silent. Finally she whispered, "Like a painting. She looks like a painting at the museum.

"Shoot," she went on, "that one's not going to be no Miss Cranberry Bog. That old Helen Margaret, she could be Miss *World*."

*   *   *

Robert, with his hair blown dry, was reading *Esquire* magazine. Bambie was under a dryer, with her red hair twisted around a billion plastic rollers. Helen Margaret, her hair dry and shiny, shaped like a small curved cap, sat silently in the corner, her eyes on the floor, her hands fooling nervously with the long sleeves of her dark brown sweater. But Anastasia noticed that every now and then Helen Margaret looked up and across the room into the mirror with a pleased, amazed expression.

Now Anastasia and Henry were in the haircutting chairs. They had been bibbed and upended and their hair had been washed.

"You ever cut any black person's hair before?" Henry asked the old lady suspiciously.

"Black, green, purple, it's all the same to me," the old lady said. "How do you want this one, Vera?"

Aunt Vera was hovering near Henry. Anastasia felt a little jealous. She wished that Aunt Vera would hover by her and make her feel special. But Aunt Vera had only stood near her chair briefly and said, "This one needs a lot of thinning and some shape. Let's try just below the ears."

Rats. Anastasia had hoped for exquisite ears.

Now Aunt Vera was holding Henry's face in her hands and tilting it from side to side. "Henry, honey," she said after a moment, "how would you feel about spectacular? You want to go for it?"

Henry grinned. Her eyes danced. "Here we come,

Mama," she said. "Heart attack time. Sure, let's go for spectacular."

Aunt Vera nodded, pleased. "Take it all off," she said to the old lady who stood there with her scissors poised.

Anastasia Krupnik

My Chosen Career

There are a lot of traumatic things you have to go through in order to achieve the kind of poise and appearance necessary for a successful bookstore owner.

First, you have to learn to look people straight in the eye and to speak distinctly. This ability will serve you very well when someone wants to return a book with coffee stains. You will be able to look them in the eye and say distinctly, "This book has coffee stains on it, you turkey. Of course I won't give you your money back."

Next, you have to have your hair styled so that you look like a different and more attractive person. If somebody wants to buy a book that costs thirty-five dollars, they probably won't buy it from someone who has long, straggly hair. So even if you have always felt at home with long, straggly hair, you need to have it thinned and shaped.

8

"Okay, everybody," Anastasia announced to her family that evening, "I want you all sitting in a row, right here on the couch. Turn that light on, Mom. The lighting needs to be right."

Mrs. Krupnik leaned over and flicked the light switch. She peered at Anastasia. "Are you wearing rouge?" she asked suspiciously. "Your cheeks look awfully pink to me. Either you're wearing rouge or you have a fever."

"Why do you still have your hat on?" Sam asked. "You're spozed to take your hat off when you come in the house."

Dr. Krupnik looked at his watch. "How long do we have to sit here, Anastasia?" he asked. "I want to watch the sports news. The Celtics won last night."

Anastasia glared at him. "Which is more important, Dad?" she asked. "The Boston Celtics, or your very own thirteen-year-old daughter's self-image?"

He opened his mouth to speak.

"Don't answer that," Anastasia said hastily, remembering her father's passion for the Celtics.

She waited until the three of them — her mother, father, and brother — were all arranged comfortably on the couch. Then she reached for her ski hat.

"Ta DA!" she said, and pulled the hat off.

Sam grinned and clapped his hands. Her mother stared in amazement.

"I'll be darned," said Dr. Krupnik. "You look like one of the Beatles, back when they were young!"

"*Daaaad*," Anastasia wailed.

"I *loved* the Beatles twenty years ago," her father added quickly. "I watched them on *The Ed Sullivan Show* on TV. I thought they were terrific-looking. And you are too, Anastasia."

"You really are, Anastasia," her mother said. "That's a wonderful haircut. I wonder why it never occurred to me that your hair would look so good cut short. My goodness, you look — "

"Older?" asked Anastasia hopefully.

"Yes. Definitely older."

"Prettier?" Anastasia smoothed her new haircut with her hands.

Her mother nodded. "Prettier. Of course I always thought you were pretty, anyway."

"Me, too," said Sam. "I was always pretty, too, wasn't I? I have pretty curls."

Anastasia ignored her brother, who was patting his own curly head. "I thought maybe they'd want to give me a perm, Mom," she said, "and I was mentally preparing myself for curls. But Aunt Vera — she's the lady in charge — she could *see* that I wasn't the curly type.

79

And she was right, wasn't she, Mom? See how it hangs down all flat? I think it's kind of sophisticated-looking."

"It is," her mother agreed. "I like the way it falls forward there over your ears."

"Please," Dr. Krupnik said, "may I go watch the sports news on TV?"

Over dinner, Anastasia described the hair-styling session.

"This girl Bambie? The one with the 'e'? She started out with curly red hair and she ended up with curly red hair, and she hadn't changed at all. But me, look how I changed!"

Everyone nodded. "Could you pour me a little more coffee, Katherine?" Anastasia's father said. "I'm going to be up late correcting exams so I might as well stock up on caffeine."

"Do you really have to work all evening?" Mrs. Krupnik asked as she added coffee to his cup. "I wanted you to watch *Nova* with me. It's all about creativity."

"And Robert? Stupid Robert Giannini? He got all nervous because he doesn't have facial hair yet. And he looked like such a jerk after he had his shampoo, because you have to wear a big bib, and lie there with your feet sticking straight out, but —"

"Excuse me, would you?" Her father stood up. "That's fascinating, Anastasia. But I really have to go and start on those exams. I'll try to take an hour off for *Nova*, Katherine." He headed for his study with the coffee cup in his hand.

"And this girl Helen Margaret! Mom, she had all this hair in her face, so you couldn't even tell what she looked like. I mean she might have had a face full of zits, and nobody would have *known!* But she didn't! They cut her hair real short, and all of a sudden she looked like — well, let me think, maybe Isabella Rossellini. Talk about *beautiful!* She still hangs her head and doesn't talk much, but you can *tell* that she really likes the way she looks, Mom. She kept peeking in the mirror and smiling —"

"Can I be excused?" asked Sam, squirming in his chair. "I want to play trucks."

Mrs. Krupnik nodded, and Sam scampered away.

"And wait till you hear this, Mom. My friend Henry? The one I told you about?"

"Is that rouge, Anastasia? Tell the truth." Her mother was looking intently at Anastasia's face.

"Just a little. We did make-up in the afternoon. All except Robert and Bambie. Did I tell you about that?" Anastasia chortled. "Robert and Bambie had to go in the other room for Diet Counseling. Of course Robert wouldn't have done make-up anyway; I mean he's a jerk, but not even Robert is *that* much of a jerk, that he'd wear make-up. But, Mom, the *thin* people — me and Helen Margaret and Henry — we got to do make-up, and the *others* — Robert and Bambie — had to go listen to a diet and exercise lecture. From Uncle Charley, of all people: one of the fattest men in the whole world!"

"It looks awfully pink to me, Anastasia. I don't think you ought to wear it to school."

School? Anastasia hadn't even thought about school

since last Friday afternoon. Why did mothers always have to mention stuff like *school?*

"Would you please listen? Forget the rouge. I promise I won't wear it to school. I want to tell you about my friend Henry."

Her mother began to clear the table. "Help me with the dishes, would you? And you can tell me about Henry then."

Typical, Anastasia thought. Try to tell a parent about the most interesting thing in the whole world, and they ask you to help with the dishes. Reluctantly she stacked up the four empty dinner plates and followed her mother to the kitchen, still talking about Henry Peabody. What had happened to Henry Peabody that day was certainly, in Anastasia's opinion, the most interesting thing in the world.

First of all, the gray-haired lady had followed Aunt Vera's instructions and had taken it *all off*. Henry's hair, that is. First the green butterfly barrettes were removed and dropped onto the linoleum floor.

"Hey, watch it, will you?" Henry said. "Don't just throw a person's personal stuff on the floor."

"Honey," Aunt Vera told her, "those butterflies are going into permanent hibernation."

Then the old lady started in with the scissors. Not snip, snip, snip, as she had done with Helen Margaret. But whack. Whack. Whack. Huge hunks of Henry Peabody's hair dropped to the floor until in no time at all the butterflies were hidden under the pile.

Within moments — Anastasia was watching out of the corner of her eye because watching Henry's haircut was even more interesting than watching her own in the mirror — Henry's hair was clipped back into a rough, thick halo around her head.

She saw Henry scowl at her own reflection. "You said spectacular," Henry bellowed, "but you're not *doing* spectacular. You're doing *ugly!*"

"Trust us, sweetie," Aunt Vera reassured her. "This is just step one." She tilted Henry's head from side to side. "This is one great-shaped head," she announced. "Take it right down to the contour," she instructed the old lady. "Let's let that contour show."

Anastasia stared glumly at herself in the mirror. Her haircut was progressing slowly; the woman was meticulously trimming it section by section. And Anastasia could see that it was going to look okay. But Aunt Vera had pronounced Helen Margaret's ears exquisite. And now she had said "great-shaped head" about Henry.

Anastasia wished — no, more than wished; she *yearned* — for Aunt Vera to say something in superlatives about her. They had studied superlatives in English class at school. Often a superlative ended in "est." Like "loveliest" or "grandest."

Anastasia wished that Aunt Vera would say, looking at her, "That is the loveliest hair."

Or sometimes a superlative began with the word "most." Like "most brilliant" or "most magnificent."

That would have been okay, too. "You have the most magnificent hair," Aunt Vera could say, hovering around Anastasia's chair.

But she didn't. She had run through one list of superlatives for Helen Margaret, and she was trotting out a whole new vocabulary of superlatives for Henry.

"The most glorious head I've seen in a long time," Aunt Vera said, watching as the old lady got out a buzzing electric thing and began to zzzzzzz Henry's head.

"You electrocute me and you die," Henry announced, but she wasn't scowling any more. She was watching herself in the mirror with a look of wonder.

And Henry was finished, even before Anastasia's beautician snipped her way around to Anastasia's left ear. All of Henry's hair except for a soft, even covering like a black fur cap was on the floor. The third old lady appeared from nowhere with a broom and swept it into a dustpan.

"You want to save these barrettes?" she asked.

Henry didn't answer at first. She was staring at herself, turning her head from side to side. Her brown ears, each with a tiny gold earring, lay flat against her perfect oval head. Her cheekbones showed. Slowly she began to smile: a tiny smile at first, just twitching her lips. Then the smile became broader as if she couldn't hold it back, and finally her small, white, even teeth showed in a wide, beautiful grin.

She glanced at the old lady holding the grubby plastic dustpan. She glanced at the four green butterflies lying on the mound of hair.

"Toss 'em," Henry said with disdain.

"I was really feeling kind of sorry for myself," Anastasia explained to her mother after she described Henry's haircut, "because even though I could see my hair was going to look good, and *I* was going to look good — and older, and prettier — I could see that I wasn't going to be beautiful. I was feeling sorry for myself about that — "

Her mother interrupted her. "You are beautiful, Anastasia, in your own way," she said.

"No, Mom. I'm okay-looking. Not a dog or anything. But let's face it, I'm not ever going to be a knockout. All of us Krupniks, we're just nice ordinary-looking people. I was kind of hoping that some miracle would happen when my hair was cut, and it didn't. But you know, it happened for Henry. I stopped feeling sorry for myself the instant I saw it happen for Henry. Because she really wants to be a model, Mom, so she can earn money to go to college. And I don't. Because I'll go to college, anyway. So she was the one who *needed* the miracle. And she got it! Isn't that a terrific thing?"

Mrs. Krupnik nodded. She wiped her hands on a dish towel and smoothed Anastasia's new, smoother, shorter hair. "You know, Anastasia," she said, "you are a truly nice, nice person."

"Could you rephrase that as a superlative, Mom?"

Her mother thought. "You are the nicest person I know," she said. "How's that?"

Anastasia grinned. "Fine. Thank you." She hung up

her own dish towel. "I'm going up to my room to rewrite the beginning of my career paper.

"Boy," she added, as she left the kitchen, "I sure hope her mother didn't *really* have a heart attack."

My Chosen Career

Some of the nicest people in the world are bookstore owners.

Other extremely nice people should not be bookstore owners because they can have a whole other glamorous career. People who have gloriously shaped heads and bony cheekbones and nice, white, even teeth should not be bookstore owners because instead they can be successful models with their pictures on magazine covers.

Then they can earn enough money to go to college. Maybe, after college, when they are old, they can be bookstore owners.

I guess I am not one of those glamorous people, though.

9

The phone rang while Anastasia's parents were watching *Nova* on TV.

"Hi! I found your number in the phone book. You're the only Krupnik!"

Anastasia recognized Henry's voice. "Hi, Henry!" she said. "Is your mom okay? She didn't have a heart attack or anything?"

Henry laughed. "She made me wash the rouge off, is all."

"All mothers are alike," Anastasia said. "I bet all mothers hate make-up on thirteen-year-olds."

"Maybe not all," Henry said. "I bet anything Bambie's mother *buys* her make-up."

"Yeah." Anastasia laughed.

"I called to see if maybe you could come have dinner at my house tomorrow night. We could go home together on the T, and then my dad can drive you to your house afterward. He said he wouldn't mind."

"Great! I'd like that," Anastasia said. "I'll check with my parents. I'm sure they'll say okay."

"I'll see you in the morning, then. It's gonna be boring tomorrow. Walking and talking, big deal. A *robot* can walk and talk."

"Yeah. Yuck." Wednesday's schedule at Studio Charmante called for lessons and practice in posture and distinct speech. It *did* sound boring.

"You wanta have lunch at McDonald's like we did today?"

"Sure. Oh, wait! I forgot."

"Forgot what? You can eat lunch. You didn't have to go to diet class with those tubs Robert and Bambie."

"I know, but I forgot that I promised to have lunch with someone. But, Henry —"

"What?"

"I bet anything she wouldn't mind if I brought you along. I'll call her and ask."

After Anastasia hung up and got an okay from her parents for dinner at the Peabodys' the next night, she dialed the bookstore owner and asked permission to bring her friend for lunch.

"Of course! Terrific!" Barbara Page said. "I love having company."

"I'm afraid she won't be able to buy a book," Anastasia explained apologetically. "She's studying to become a model so that she can earn the money to go to college, so —"

"Hey," Barbara Page interrupted, laughing. "I said I love having company. I didn't mean I love having customers."

* * *

"Whaddaya mean, she had an autographing party for your father? Is your father a rock star or something?"

Anastasia shook her head. They were walking across the Common toward Beacon Hill. "He's just a college professor. But he writes poetry, too."

"Real poetry? In books? Not just funny poems for uncles' birthday parties and stuff?"

Anastasia nodded. "No. Of course he does that, too. But he writes real poetry. In books."

"Jeezum," said Henry. "Real books. Do they have his name on them?"

"Sure. Right across the front. And they have his picture on the back."

Henry looked awed. "So he's famous," she said.

Anastasia felt embarrassed. She didn't think of her father as famous. Still, every now and then, they wrote about him in the *New York Times*. Once they had called him "Master of the Contemporary Image," whatever that meant. And strangers wrote fan letters to him, asking for his autograph. So she guessed he was famous, at least a little.

"Yeah," she admitted. "I guess so."

"I never once in my whole entire life knew the daughter of a famous person before," Henry said.

Anastasia tried to think of a response. "I never knew a truly beautiful person before," she said, finally. "In fact, when I first knew you, just two days ago, I didn't even recognize that you were beautiful. And now look. Do you realize, Henry, that right now, right this very minute, as we walk through the Common, men are star-

90

ing at you because you're so beautiful? *Grown men?*"

"Yeah, I know. It's weird. Last night, when I was going home on the T, men stared at me. *Women* even stared at me. That never happened to me before."

"Is it scary?"

Henry shook her head. "No. Not if they just stare. But if they *say* anything, they die."

And Barbara Page stared, too, when they entered the bookstore. She stared at both of them as Anastasia introduced her to Henry.

"Anastasia," she said, "your haircut is fabulous, and I want you to give me the name of the person who cut it, because I want to make an appointment.

"And, Henry," she went on, "*you* are gorgeous. There's no other word for it."

"Yes, there is," Anastasia told her in surprise. "You of all people — a person who owns a bookstore — ought to know that. There are *lots* of other words for it. Dazzling. Spectacular. Magnificent. Just plain *beautiful,* for pete's sake."

"Okay, okay." Barbara Page laughed. "You're right."

"Wanta see what we learned at modeling school this morning?" Henry asked.

"Sure. Show me."

Henry dropped her jacket on a bench in a corner of the bookstore. She posed, standing straight; then she took a deep breath and walked across the floor to the opposite wall of bookcases. Her chin was high, her shoulders taut, and her long legs moved with a kind of grace that Anastasia had never seen on anyone before.

91

Instead of hanging at her sides like every other pair of arms in the whole world, Henry Peabody's arms moved with a fluid ease. She turned, smiled slowly, and strode back toward them with the same gliding movement.

Then she grinned. "Whaddaya think?" Henry asked. "Panther, or what?"

"Panther," Anastasia said. "For sure."

Aunt Vera had directed them, in class, to imagine themselves as animals. After they had finished goofing off and acting stupid because they were all so embarrassed, they had tried.

Bambie had chosen a mountain goat. Mountain goats, Bambie explained, would have a determined, sure-footed walk. Then she mountain-goated across the room with her red curls bouncing. Ho hum.

Helen Margaret had hung her head and said softly, "I'll try to be a deer, I guess." She walked timidly across the room, darting looks at Aunt Vera to see if she was doing it right. She *did* resemble a deer, Anastasia thought, remembering a deer she had seen once at the edge of a meadow; Helen Margaret had the same fearful, shy look, the same careful steps, the same vigilance.

Robert went next. "Cheetah," he announced, which was a joke before he even started. There was no way that Robert Giannini could look like a cheetah. He clumped across the room; Aunt Vera smiled a polite but pained smile, and Henry muttered under her breath, "Make that hippo."

"Ah, well, I guess I'll try lioness," Anastasia said when her turn came. She walked across the room, imagining

92

herself stalking game on the African veldt. But she tripped on an untied shoelace and started to laugh. "I meant giraffe," she said.

Henry had simply said "Panther," and then she had panthered herself across the room so magnificently that everyone — even Bambie — burst into applause.

Now she had done it again in the bookstore. She *became* a panther somehow.

"This afternoon," Anastasia told Barbara Page, "we practice speaking. I think I can do that better than walking."

"If Bambie Browne does her Juliet death scene again," Henry said, and she imitated Bambie, " 'to whose foul mouth no healthsome air breathes in,' well, you might just hear a foul mouth make a comment. And it'll be mine."

Barbara Page made a tsk-tsking sound, but Anastasia could see she was laughing silently.

Over a lunch of egg salad sandwiches, Anastasia said, "You know, the modeling course is actually kind of fun. The haircuts and make-up day was a whole lot of fun. And this morning wasn't bad, even if I did turn out to be a giraffe."

"You should try panther," Henry commented, shaking some pepper onto her egg salad.

Anastasia made a face. "I don't think I'm pantherlike, Henry. I'm too klutzy. Anyway, I like giraffes."

"I like giraffes, too," Barbara Page said. "My husband and I went on safari in Africa last year, and we saw a lot of giraffes."

Henry's eyes widened. "Safari?" she said. "Africa?"

"Who ran the bookstore while you were away?" Anastasia asked.

Barbara looked a little embarrassed. "I just closed it down," she said. "I probably should have hired someone to come in and take charge. But I didn't trust anybody to know how to handle all the senior citizens and the little kids and all my customers that I know so well. So when I go on vacation, I just lock up the shop."

"You need to train an assistant," Anastasia suggested.

"Maybe."

"A young assistant," Anastasia said.

"I suppose so."

"Someone like *me*," Anastasia said.

Barbara smiled. "That's a good thought," she said. "Maybe next summer we can discuss a part-time job for you. And then eventually, when you're older, I could leave you in charge, and my husband and I could go to Africa again. I'd love to go back.

"As a matter of fact," she said suddenly, "when you came in here, Henry, you reminded me of something — or someone — and I couldn't put my finger on what it was. But I just realized. Look." She walked over to the section marked TRAVEL and reached for a large book. She leafed through its pages, found what she wanted, and turned to show the photograph to Henry and Anastasia.

"Jeezum," Henry said softly. "My haircut." She took the book from Barbara Page and sat down.

Anastasia peered over Henry's shoulder and looked at

the portrait of the Masai woman. She was wrapped in a red blanket and had large, beaded necklaces around her throat and rings of beads dangling from her ears. Her head was shaved down to a thin layer of hair, the same as Henry's, and she had Henry's high cheekbones, slender neck, and large dark eyes.

"I saw a lot of women who looked just like her — and you — in Kenya and Tanzania," Barbara Page said. "They were all very beautiful."

Henry closed the book slowly and laid it on the desk. She looked worried. "You don't think they'll all come over here and go to modeling school?" she asked. "I don't think I can deal with all that competition."

Barbara Page laughed. "I don't think so," she said.

"Can I look at the children's books?" Henry asked. "I got two little nephews who like books."

"Sure. Go through the ones on the little table, and if you find one you want, you can have it. The nursery school comes in here for story hour, and the kids have dirty hands sometimes. So those books have some smears, and I can't sell them."

While Henry was leafing through the children's books on the table, Anastasia sat down beside Barbara Page's desk and spoke softly. "I told you I wanted to buy a book," she began.

Barbara Page laughed. "Don't be silly. Take one of those kids' books home for your brother — no charge. I'm not going to take your money."

"No, wait," Anastasia whispered. "I really want to. But I didn't know which book I wanted. And now I do.

I want to buy that one." She indicated the book on the desk. "I want to buy it for Henry, so she can look again and again at how beautiful the Masai woman is."

Barbara Page smiled. "I'm sorry, Anastasia. But it's not for sale. It's already spoken for."

"*Rats.*"

The telephone rang. "Could you answer that, Anastasia, and practice being a bookstore owner? Get it in the front room. I have some stuff to tend to in here."

Anastasia nodded and went to the front of the bookstore where another telephone was on the wall. "Pages, good afternoon," she said, remembering how Barbara Page always answered the phone. Henry, sitting at the children's table, looked over at her and grinned.

"Barbara?" a woman's voice asked.

"No," Anastasia answered, "Mrs. Page is busy at the moment. This is her assistant. May I help you?" She crossed her fingers, hoping the woman had a question she would be able to answer.

"Well, I'm looking for a gift for a friend. Could you recommend something? Nonfiction, I think."

Anastasia glanced quickly at the shelves. She saw cookbooks, gardening books, biographies, travel books, photography books.

"Well, ah, what are your friend's interests?" she asked.

"She's quite literary," the woman responded. "She's the librarian at a boys' boarding school."

Suddenly Anastasia's eyes fastened on a particular section of the shelves.

"In that case," she said into the telephone, "she would

appreciate an autographed edition. And we just happen to have here an autographed copy of the latest volume of Myron Krupnik's poetry."

"Myron Krupnik? Have I heard of him?"

"I should hope so," Anastasia said. "The *New York Times* called him 'Master of the Contemporary Image.'"

"Goodness. Well, I think she *would* like that. You say it's autographed?"

"It certainly is. He has terrible handwriting, but lots of famous people have terrible handwriting. I know someone who got Bruce Springsteen's autograph once, and Bruce Springsteen had terri —"

"Yes, well, could you gift wrap that and mail it for me? I'll give you the address and you can charge it to my account."

Anastasia copied down the information carefully. Then she took it triumphantly to the back room, where Barbara Page was still at her desk. "I sold a book!" she said.

"No kidding!" Barbara Page looked delighted.

"My own father's book! She wants you to mail it to her friend. Here's the address."

"Anastasia, I think you have a great future as a bookstore owner. Thank you. Now, here — it's almost one o'clock. You guys have to go back and practice talking. Not that you seem to have any trouble with it, either one of you." She handed Anastasia and Henry each a paper bag with PAGES printed on the side in wide blue letters.

"What's this?" Anastasia asked.

"A present for each of you. And a few smeary books for your little brothers and nephews."

She walked them to the door with an arm around each of them. "Come back and see me again, okay?"

"Okay, and thank you," Henry and Anastasia said.

Outside, walking back through the Common, they looked inside their shopping bags. Anastasia found a book about trucks for Sam and a book for herself which contained beautiful color photographs of animals. Inside the front cover, Barbara Page had written, "For my friend and future bookstore owner, Anastasia Krupnik. Giraffes are my very favorite. With love from Barbara Page."

Henry pulled out the two picture books she had chosen for her nephews and the book that contained the picture of the Masai woman. Inside, Barbara Page had written, "For Henrietta Peabody, who comes from a long tradition of great beauty."

Henry held it out, looking stricken.

"Anastasia," she said, "I saw the price on this book. It was thirty-five dollars!"

"Well," Anastasia said, thinking it over, "she wanted you to have it. Like my father said, she's a terrific person. And she can afford it. But boy, she sure is a terrible bookstore owner, though.

"Oh, no!" she added, remembering something. "Oh, rats! I forgot to do the interview again!"

But Henry wasn't listening. She was turning the pages of the book slowly. She found the Masai woman, stared at her silently as they walked, and then turned back to the inscription again. "I sure am glad," she said finally, "that she wrote my real name: Henrietta."

Anastasia Krupnik

My Chosen Career

It really is not all that difficult being a bookstore owner. If someone calls up and asks you to recommend a book, it is really pretty easy to convince them to buy something, like maybe a book by a moderately successful poet,* just by speaking pleasantly to them about it. Of course, if they come into the store, you have to look them in the eye at the same time.

One of the problems with being a bookstore owner, if you are a terrifically nice person, is that you are tempted to give stuff away.

If you sell a book by a moderately successful poet* for $12.95, and on the same day give away a book that costs $35, you will be a terrible failure as a bookstore owner even though you would still be a terrifically nice person.

You could solve this by selling the $35 book and giving away the $12.95 book. That way, you would still be a terrifically nice person, and you could also be a moderately successful bookstore owner.

*Myron Krupnik, Ph.D.

10

"I've never been in Dorchester before," Anastasia said to Henry as they sat side by side on the rattling subway. "Imagine that. All my life I've lived in Boston but I've never been in that part of Boston before."

"Well, shoot, that's no surprise," Henry said. "All my life *I've* lived in Boston and I've never been to the suburbs where you live, either."

"Maybe you could come to my house sometime. You'd like my family."

"What're they like? I know your dad is famous and all. But what're your parents really like?"

"Well, my dad has a really neat beard. It's the same color as my hair. And he tells terrible jokes, and he watches sports on TV. When he's working on a book of poetry he shuts himself up in the study and groans about how he should have chosen another career."

"That's so cool," said Henry. "In school, I always like when we study poems. And now that we learned about walking and talking and stuff, I bet I'll do really good when we have to recite. Shoot, maybe I'll do gestures, like Miss Cranberry Bog."

They both collapsed in giggles, and an elderly lady sitting nearby stared at them. No men were staring at Henry, but that was because she had her hat on. If she took her hat off, Anastasia knew, she would change to beautiful in about the same way that Clark Kent changed to Superman. *Then* men would stare at her.

"And my mom's an artist," Anastasia went on. "She works at home, so she can take care of my little brother at the same time. She illustrates books."

"My mom's a waitress. That's the hardest job in the whole world. You should see how her feet swell up. She has to soak them when she comes home. Boy, I'm never going to be a waitress."

"Well, of course not, Henry. You're going to be a model."

"Yeah." Suddenly Henry sat up very straight and removed her hat. Two men sitting together on the opposite side of the train stopped talking, nudged each other, and stared.

"Just testing," Henry remarked in a whisper to Anastasia, and grinned. She put her hat back on and slouched down again.

"What does your dad do?" Anastasia asked.

"Policeman."

"No kidding! Does he have a *gun?*"

"Whaddaya mean does he have a gun? Of *course* he

has a gun. You think he wants to be the only cop in Boston with no gun?"

"Did he ever shoot anyone?" Anastasia asked in awe.

Henry shook her head. "Nope. Never once. Once he had to aim it at somebody, though. It gave him nightmares afterward."

Anastasia shuddered. Never in her whole life, she thought, had she known someone whose father had once aimed a gun at someone.

"We get off here," Henry announced as the train slowed and stopped. Anastasia followed her through the subway station and out into the street.

The Peabodys' house, two blocks away, was gray, a little in need of new paint, with a big front porch. Inside, it smelled of something delicious cooking. And it was noisy. Two small children ran giggling through the front hall as the girls were taking off their jackets and hats. Henry grabbed one of them by the shoulders, and the other stopped, stood still, and looked up shyly at Anastasia.

"These are my sister's kids," Henry explained. "It's my mom's day off, so she's babysitting. This evil one's Jason." She wiggled the arm of the one she was restraining, and the little boy grinned. "And that one there, that's John Peter. Say hi, you guys."

John Peter opened his mouth, his eyes wide, and whispered, "Hi." Jason squirmed loose from Henry's grasp and stuck out his tongue. Then they both ran off, laughing.

"Henrietta? Is that you?" a voice called.

Henry hung up her jacket and called, "Yes, Mom. I have Anastasia with me. We'll be right in."

"You walk in here normal, Henrietta," her mother called. "None of that panther stuff."

Anastasia followed Henry into the warm kitchen, where the two little boys were now tussling on the floor and Mrs. Peabody stood at the stove stirring something steamy in a large pot. She turned and shook Anastasia's hand when Henry introduced them.

"Now look at that nice haircut you have," she said. "I just don't know what to make of Henrietta's. Seems as if they just shaved her down to nothing."

"But don't you think it's beautiful?" Anastasia asked.

Mrs. Peabody frowned, looking at her daughter. "I have to get used to it, I guess," she said. Then she called to her grandchildren. "Jason! John Peter! You settle down now! We have company! You want Anastasia to think we're raising wild animals here?"

The little boys ignored her and continued tickling each other and shrieking with laughter.

"Henrietta, you go wake up your daddy and tell him dinner's almost ready." Henry left the kitchen and Mrs. Peabody turned back to the stove. "He's working the night shift this week, so he slept all day. He's going to take you home when he leaves to go to work," she explained to Anastasia. "Sit down and make yourself comfortable."

Anastasia took a chair at the big kitchen table. It felt something like her own house: the warm, friendly, good-smelling kitchen; the little boys, just Sam's size, playing on the floor; the potholder mitten hanging from a magnet on the refrigerator door. She noticed a teapot shaped like a little house, exactly like a teapot that her own mother had.

Wait till I tell Mom, she thought, about how a black family here in Dorchester has a teapot exactly like ours. I thought we were the only people in the whole world with that teapot.

Wait till I tell Mom and Dad and Sam that Henry's father is a policeman — just like Bobby Hill on *Hill Street Blues* — and that once he actually aimed a gun at someone.

Suddenly Anastasia had a terrifying thought. Henry's father was going to take her home on his way to work. That meant that she — Anastasia Krupnik — would be driven right up her own driveway in a police car. Maybe the blue lights would be flashing. She would be riding with someone who had a gun in a holster on his hip. The police radio would be on. What if a call came in — an *emergency* — and he had to stop along the way and arrest a criminal? Then she — Anastasia Krupnik — would be riding in the police car, probably in the back seat, and there would be a metal grille separating her from Henry's father, and she would be sitting beside a hardened criminal. Of course the criminal would be in handcuffs. But maybe, even with the handcuffs on, he could grab her. Take her hostage. He could say to Henry's father, through the grille, "Unlock these handcuffs or I will kill this thirteen-year-old girl."

Then Mr. Peabody would *do* it, of course. Mr. Peabody

was the kind of guy who had nightmares after he aimed his gun at someone. So of course out of concern for Anastasia's life he would have to stop the car and unlock the handcuffs.

Then Anastasia would be in the clutches of an unhandcuffed hardened criminal.

It wouldn't be Henry's father's *fault*, she thought sadly, feeling terribly sorry, partly for him, because he would be stricken with the helplessness and guilt, but mostly for herself and the fate that lay in store.

Probably Mr. Peabody would aim his gun at the guy. But she — Anastasia Krupnik, innocent victim — would be in *front* of the criminal. He would have one arm around her neck; maybe the other would be holding a knife to her throat.

I suppose Henry's father could radio for a SWAT team, she thought, the way they sometimes did on TV. She wasn't exactly certain, though, what a SWAT team was or what it was supposed to do. Heck, if they just came and swatted at the criminal — the way her mother sometimes swatted at Sam's behind when he was being naughty — what good would *that* do?

Anastasia stared glumly at the teapot that was just like her mother's and wondered whether she would ever see her mother's teapot again. She wondered whether she would ever get to Thursday's classes at Studio Charmante. Thursday was Fashion Consultation. Anastasia *needed* Fashion Consultation. Everybody else in the class would be getting Fashion Consultation, and she — Anastasia Krupnik, innocent victim — would probably be bound and gagged in a deserted warehouse someplace, still wearing these same old jeans.

Her thoughts, which had become sadder and sadder, were interrupted when Henry reappeared. "This is my dad," Henry said cheerfully. "Dad, this is my friend Anastasia."

Anastasia looked up. Mr. Peabody smiled and reached out his hand to shake hers. He wasn't wearing a gun. He wasn't even wearing a uniform. He was wearing corduroy pants, just like her father's, and a dark green sweater.

"Hi," he said. "I'm glad to meet you, Anastasia."

"I'm glad to meet you, too," she said. Then she gulped. "I, ah, I don't know what to call you. Is it Officer Peabody?"

He laughed. "How about Frank?" he suggested. "That's my name."

"I have a *goldfish* named Frank!" Anastasia exclaimed.

Oh, *great*, she thought instantly. Talk about *dumb*. Telling a policeman that your goldfish has his name.

But Frank Peabody was laughing. So was his wife. So was Henry.

"Guess what!" Anastasia burst through the door to her father's study. Her parents both looked up from their books.

"What?" they asked in unison.

"A policeman brought me home! But he wasn't wearing a gun, and he wasn't in a police car — it was just an old car like ours, Dad, and he said it always needs lots of repairs, same as ours — so there were no blue lights

106

flashing and no radio. Well, yes, there *was* a radio, but I meant that it wasn't a *police* radio, so there weren't any emergency calls, and we didn't have to stop and arrest anyone, and he wasn't wearing a uniform because he changes at the station — "

Her parents looked concerned. "Hold it," her father said. "Slow down. What do you mean, a policeman brought you home? I thought your friend's father was bringing you home."

"Henry's father is a policeman! Isn't that *neat?* Just like Bobby Hill. *Exactly* like Bobby Hill. He even *looks* like Bobby Hill! But he has never *once* shot anyone. He only aimed his gun one time, and after that he had nightmares.

"And her mother," Anastasia went on, "is a waitress. Poor Mrs. Peabody, her feet get so swollen from being a waitress that she has to soak them when she gets home, but tonight she wasn't soaking them, because today was her day off, so today she was babysitting for these cute little boys; one is named Jason, and one is named John Peter — "

She paused to take a breath. "And we had pot roast, and it was delicious. Mom, it was even better than your pot roast, because Mrs. Peabody's pot roast gravy doesn't have one single lump in it. Not even one tiny lump; do you believe that? She says that the secret is to blend the flour in real slowly, with a fork, and never stop stirring, not for one single second.

"And you know what else? I forgot to do my interview again, but it doesn't really matter, because Barbara Page

107

is the world's worst bookstore owner — she gives stuff away all the time; wait till you see what she gave me, and wait till you hear what she gave Henry — and she let me answer the phone, and I sold a book, and wait till you hear what book I sold. You'll really freak!

"And tomorrow is Fashion Consultation! I thought I'd miss it because I thought I'd be in an abandoned warehouse with old rags stuffed in my mouth so I couldn't even scream, but I'm *not!* So I get to go to Fashion Consultation tomorrow! And you should have seen me this morning, Mom and Dad, when we practiced walking, because I was just like a giraffe; it was soooo funny! Barbara Page says that giraffes are her favorites, and she ought to know, because she went on safari in Africa—"

Anastasia flopped down on the couch, exhausted.

"And I haven't even told you yet about the amazing coincidence of the teapot," she added.

Dr. Krupnik pushed back the sleeve of his sweater and looked at his watch. "Katherine," he said, "it's ten o'clock. Do you know where your children are?"

Katherine Krupnik shook her head slowly. "The little one's in bed," she said. "But the other? I haven't the foggiest idea."

"Ha ha," Anastasia said. "The *other* one is headed up to her bedroom to rewrite her school assignment for the ninth time."

My Chosen Career

There are a lot of good things about being a bookstore owner that you might not be aware of until you have done a lot of research.

1. Men don't stare at you.
2. Your feet don't get all swollen up and you don't have to soak them.
3. You don't have to carry a gun.
4. Or a briefcase.

11

"Do you think this is an okay outfit to wear on the day we're having Fashion Consultation, Mom?" Anastasia stood beside the kitchen table at breakfast, and posed. She was wearing clean jeans and a dark blue sweat shirt that said SKI YOUR BUNS OFF across the chest. "This shirt is sort of a lie because I don't even ski. But it's one of my favorites."

"Sure. I don't think it matters what you wear because they'll want to start from scratch. It's like going to the beauty parlor. You don't trim your own hair first. You let them start from square one."

Anastasia's father looked up from the newspaper. "I've been trying to tell you that for years, Katherine," he said. "You always clean the house the day before the cleaning lady comes. That makes no sense at all."

"Of course it makes sense," Katherine Krupnik said. "I don't want her to think I'm a slob."

"That's right, Mom," Anastasia agreed. "And I don't want Aunt Vera and Uncle Charley to think I'm a slob."

She looked down at herself. Like all of her jeans, these had patches. Her sweat shirt had frayed cuffs. "Of course I *am* a slob — that's the whole trouble," she said.

"No, you're not," her mother told her. "When you're dressed up, you look great. And those clothes aren't slobbish — they're just casual. You look fine. Really."

Relieved, Anastasia sat down and began to eat.

The main room at Studio Charmante was arranged differently that morning. The chairs were set up in a semicircle, and several large mirrors were propped against the walls. All five kids — even Helen Margaret — kept looking at themselves in the mirrors. It was hard not to.

Aunt Vera talked for a while about colors and color combinations and different styles of clothing. She held up a lot of pictures illustrating Casual (but it was tweed and cashmere, not at all what Anastasia's mother had told her was casual), Sophisticated, Executive Look, Fun and Far-Out. It was all pretty boring.

But then the interesting part started. A woman wearing Executive Look — a dark gray suit and a cream-colored silk blouse — arrived, and Aunt Vera introduced her as Fashion Coordinator from Filene's. Her name was Sarah Silverman.

Anastasia liked that. She always liked names with matching consonants, like her mother's: Katherine Krupnik. She could never figure out why her parents hadn't given her a name that began with "K." Kim, maybe. Kimberly Krupnik. Instead of, yuck, Anastasia.

Even matching *ending* consonants would be okay, she thought. Like Henry Peabody: those two matching "y's" at the end of her two names really gave it a neat sound.

Anastasia tried to think of a name that ended in "k," a

111

first name that would go with Krupnik.

Rick. Rick Krupnik.

Jack. *Jack* Krupnik.

Mick, maybe. Or how about *Spike?* Like Spike Owen on the Red Sox. It didn't matter that it was a guy's name — look at Henry; she had a guy's name, and it sounded great.

Spike Krupnik. Anastasia said it to herself several times. She wondered how her parents would feel if she changed her name to Spike.

"Anastasia? Are you listening?" Sarah Silverman, the Fashion Coordinator, was leaning toward her with a questioning look.

"Oooops. Sorry. I was daydreaming, I guess," Anastasia said, embarrassed.

Sarah Silverman smiled. "I was explaining," she said, "that I've brought a variety of clothes with me from the store. Aunt Vera told me the sizes. Now I'm going to take each of you in turn and analyze your coloring and type. Then we'll try different outfits, and you'll see how your whole look can change."

"Do we get to keep the clothes?" Henry asked.

Sarah Silverman shook her head. "No. I'm sorry. But we *can* offer you a ten percent discount on the regular price, if there's anything you want to buy."

"Rats," Anastasia whispered. "I can't afford anything."

"Neither can I," Henry whispered back.

"Who wants to go first?" Sarah Silverman asked.

"ME!" Bambie Browne was already standing up.

"All right." Sarah Silverman stood beside Bambie in

front of the group. She cupped her hands around Bambie's chin and tilted her face toward the light.

"Bambie has a typical redhead's coloring," she said. "Pale skin and green eyes. We'll try a few cool colors on Bambie."

"I don't really care about looking cool," Bambie said. "In the entertainment field it's more important to look — "

"I didn't mean that kind of cool," Sarah Silverman said. "I meant blues and greens. We call those cool colors, as opposed to — well, it's complicated to explain. Trust me.

"Now," she went on, "since Bambie has a tiny weight problem — "

"We had our Diet Counseling on Tuesday," Aunt Vera explained. "And Bambie's going to start watching the calories."

Bambie blushed.

Aunt Vera took Bambie off into the dressing room. Anastasia and Henry watched, bored, as Bambie returned wearing a pair of green tweed slacks and a bulky green sweater. Actually, she *did* look pretty good dressed in the new clothes.

"Did you bring jewelry?" Bambie asked. "I'd like a whole lot of gold jewelry. When I do one of my monologues, especially in front of TV cameras, I think there should be a lot of bracelets flashing during my gestures."

"Your gestures?" Sarah Silverman asked.

Bambie demonstrated. She recited a few lines from something and her arms moved about. She looked like a puppet.

113

"Oh," said Sarah Silverman. "Well, I'm afraid I don't have jewelry with me. But I see what you mean. Probably, though, you wouldn't be wearing slacks and a sweater if you were doing a, ah, monologue on TV."

"Oh, of course not," Bambie said. "I have my costumes specially made. I have a Scarlett O'Hara outfit, and I have a Little Mary Sunshine, and I have a Poor Little Match Girl, and then of course my Juliet — "

Sarah Silverman nodded. "Well, Filene's certainly can't compete with that," she said. "But let's stick with regular clothes now, Bambie. I'm going to put a wonderful plaid coat over that outfit now. It'll look great with that red hair."

When she had finished with Bambie, she selected Robert and stood beside him.

"Now Robert, too, has to work on his weight a bit," she said. "But he has — "

Robert interrupted. "I'm expecting my growth spurt any time now," he said. "And I'll thin out then. My pediatrician told my mother I would."

Anastasia poked Henry and they both tightened their mouths to restrain their laughter.

"Great," Sarah Silverman said. "And in the meantime, Robert, you still have lovely dark hair and that wonderful, clear olive skin. Let's see how you'll look in some really smashing sportswear."

Uncle Charley led Robert off to the dressing room. Anastasia was in the middle of a yawn when he returned, and she almost choked when her yawn turned into a gasp. Robert Giannini in designer jeans, an enormous

114

red and yellow plaid shirt with huge shoulder pads, and a golf hat: it was the most astounding thing she'd ever seen.

Henry put two fingers into her mouth and gave a piercing whistle. Robert blushed, grinned, and attempted once again to do a cheetah-like walk.

Anastasia found herself hoping, for Robert's sake, that even with the 10 percent discount he couldn't afford to *buy* that outfit. It did look somewhat sensational here in the privacy of Studio Charmante. But if Robert Giannini showed up in his seventh-grade classroom wearing designer sportswear with giant shoulder pads — well, Anastasia shuddered to think what might happen.

Robert clumped about, preening, and then he said to Sarah Silverman, "What's your opinion of a *Miami Vice* look, for someone who doesn't yet have chest hair?"

Bambie was admiring her own fingernails. Helen Margaret was looking at the floor. Henry hooted loudly and grinned. But Anastasia wanted to die. It would be bad enough to hear a zoo keeper, talking about gorillas, mention chest hair, which was certainly one of the grossest things in the whole world. To hear Robert Giannini talk about chest hair was absolutely unbearable. Anastasia looked at the ceiling and tried to think about some subject that wouldn't have anything to do with chest hair. *Mr. Rogers' Neighborhood*. She thought about *Mr. Rogers' Neighborhood* as hard as she could so that she couldn't hear Sarah Silverman talking to Robert.

Finally Robert was back in his seat, wearing his own Giannini-style clothes again. In an odd way, it was reassuring to see him looking normal — even if normal meant dressed like a wimp.

"Now," Sarah Silverman said, looking around, "Helen Margaret."

Helen Margaret had been sitting silently as Bambie and Robert modeled their clothes. But now she ducked her head, wrapped her arms around herself as if for protection, and whispered, "I don't want to."

"It's fun," Bambie said. "Come on. She has a gorgeous dress hanging in there, just your size."

Helen Margaret shook her head back and forth. "No," she whimpered.

Robert turned to her. "I know how you feel," he said, "because I really felt like a jerk standing there with everyone looking at me. But you just have to laugh at yourself. It really is fun. Come on."

Everyone in the room said encouraging things until finally, reluctantly, Helen Margaret stood up. She looked terrified. Her shoulders slumped. Her eyes were on the floor.

"You're a *very* pretty girl," Sarah Silverman said in a kind voice. "And Bambie was right, that I have a gorgeous dress intended for you. Aunt Vera described each of you to me, and now that I see you, I know I've chosen just the right clothes."

Helen Margaret looked up at last. She stood woodenly, with a frightened expression, while Sarah Silverman analyzed her appearance.

"Helen Margaret is so tiny, so fragile," she said, "that one of those big shirts or sweaters would overwhelm her.

So I've chosen pastel colors and fine, delicate fabrics for her. Aunt Vera, could you take her in and help her with that pale blue dress?"

Aunt Vera took Helen Margaret by the hand and led her to the dressing room.

"When she comes out," Sarah Silverman said to the others, "she will take your breath away. It's too bad she's so shy because she has an *exquisite* look."

But suddenly they all heard noise from the dressing room. "No! Don't!" they heard Helen Margaret scream. Then they heard sobbing. "Don't! I don't want you to — Please! Stop! Don't! I can't — " The words were hard to understand because the voice was panic-stricken and hysterical, choking with sobs.

Then Helen Margaret, still dressed in the skirt and sweater she'd been wearing, ran from the dressing room. Her hands were covering her face. "You don't understand! I can't — " she gasped. She ran through the room, out the door, and disappeared.

Aunt Vera followed from the dressing room, holding the pale blue dress over her arm. "Where is she?" she asked. "I don't know what happened. She was standing there stiff as a board, and wouldn't undress, so I started to unbutton her sweater, just to help, and she seemed to go crazy. Look — she even scratched me." Aunt Vera held out her arm and showed them a long scratch with a few drops of blood oozing from it.

"She must have gone to the ladies' room," Uncle Charley said.

Aunt Vera and Sarah Silverman went to look. But in a

moment they were back, with puzzled expressions. "She's gone," Aunt Vera said. "Her coat is gone."

"Well," Uncle Charley said after a moment's silence, "she'll probably be back. Her pocketbook's still right there by her chair. Is your arm all right, Vera?"

"Oh, yeah. It's just a scratch. Listen, kids, I think we'll just continue as if nothing happened. When she gets back, let's all be real supportive and friendly. I guess we shouldn't have insisted that she try on the clothes, but I thought it would cheer her up to see how pretty she could be."

"Anastasia," Sarah Silverman said, "we'll do you next. Vera told me that you're thinking about becoming a bookstore owner someday, and I have a terrific outfit in your size: businesslike and intellectual. Just what a successful bookstore owner should wear."

Anastasia stood up. She couldn't think of anything else to do. But the cheerful excitement was gone. Sarah Silverman talked about Anastasia's coloring and style, but there was a worried hush in the room.

Suddenly Robert Giannini stood up. "Listen, you guys," he said in a loud voice, "we can't just sit here doing *nothing*. Where does she live?"

"Somerville," Uncle Charley told him. "The address is on the list on the front desk."

"Well, I'm going to try to find her," Robert said. "The rest of you stay here in case she comes back or calls. I'll look out on the street, and if she's not there I'll go to her house."

Then Robert, too, was gone.

My Chosen Career

One of the best things about being a book-store owner is that nothing embarrassing would ever happen to you.

No one would scream and cry and run outside and make you all worried.

You don't have to change your clothes in front of other people.

No one would ever come into a bookstore and talk about stuff like chest hair.

12

The day seemed endless. Anastasia dutifully tried on the clothes that Sarah Silverman had selected for her; and she could see that they looked terrific, and that *she* looked terrific, and that everyone else thought so, too. But the atmosphere had changed.

After Anastasia, Henry's turn came. Anastasia sensed that Sarah Silverman had purposely saved Henry till last because she knew how sensational the transformation would be. And it was. Even with Robert and Helen Margaret gone, and with the disconcerting worry that their absence caused, it was exciting to watch Henry model the bright-colored high-fashion clothes that Sarah Silverman had provided for her.

Tall, thin, glowing, Henry moved with her panther's stealthy, sinuous walk across the shabby, linoleum-floored room, wearing a floor-length apricot silk gown. Her dark chin high, she posed for a moment with absolute self-confidence. Then she smiled. The audience fell silent. A moment before Sarah Silverman had been describing, explaining, and instructing; now her voice fell still. Anastasia had been cracking jokes; now she couldn't speak, and she felt a shiver along her spine. Bambie stared and said nothing. Uncle Charley had been coming and going, making phone calls to Helen Margaret's number, receiving no answer; now he stood in the doorway, his arms folded across his enormous belly, and watched without a word.

Aunt Vera dabbed her eyes. "Charley," she whispered finally, "I've waited twenty years for this."

It was Henry herself who broke the spell, finally. "Shoot," she said, grinning, "you ain't seen *nuthin'* yet. Wait'll I do my monologue."

Even Bambie laughed.

But the rest of the day was dulled by concern for Helen Margaret. They all ate a take-out lunch of cold egg rolls and fried rice that Uncle Charley picked up from the Chinese restaurant across the street, and they listened as he tried again without success to reach the phone number written on the list.

"I think," Bambie suggested, "that she just felt inferior and it made her nervous. I know I felt that way once, when I was waiting to do my performance at a pageant, and the girl before me did a real good accordion solo. Maybe you should have had her go first, so she wouldn't have had to feel inferior to some of us who have more experience."

No one said anything. Bambie, who was supposed to be watching her calories, reached for another egg roll.

"I don't think I should have let Robert go off like that,"

Uncle Charley said in a worried voice. "I don't like the thought of a kid wandering around all alone in the city."

Despite her feeling of unease, Anastasia started to laugh. "Uncle Charley," she said, "you don't need to worry about Robert Giannini. I've known him for years. Robert Giannini is prepared for absolutely any emergency."

"What if he gets lost? Do you think he'd ask directions? I know kids your age don't like to ask for help."

"Uncle Charley," Anastasia reassured him, "Robert Giannini is not like other kids. Robert Giannini has no inhibitions. *None.*"

Sarah Silverman had scheduled a tour through Filene's Junior Department for the class after lunch.

"Why don't you all go ahead?" Aunt Vera said. "Charley and I will be here in case Robert and Helen Margaret get back."

So Henry, Anastasia, and Bambie followed Sarah Silverman around Filene's, looking at clothes, talking to salespeople, and watching the workmen in the back rooms building displays.

They didn't go to the Basement, where everything was marked down in price. "Is it true, Sarah," Anastasia asked, "that in the Basement people try on clothes right out in public?"

Sarah chuckled and nodded. "You want to go down there?"

"No," Anastasia said. "I'm not into underwear, especially."

"Do models work here?" Henry asked.

"We hire them for fashion shows," Sarah told her.

Henry hesitated. Then she said, "Do you think maybe sometime — I mean after I have more practice and stuff — maybe someday . . ."

Sarah Silverman grinned. "Henry Peabody," she said, "I have your phone number right here in my hot little hand. It's the most valuable thing I own at the moment. You will definitely be hearing from me."

Aunt Vera and Uncle Charley were sipping coffee and looking more relaxed when the group returned from Filene's.

"Robert called," Uncle Charley announced. "He found her."

"Where? What was wrong? Did he say?" Bambie, Henry, and Anastasia were all talking at once.

"Hey, slow down. I'll tell you what I know. He said he found her — he didn't say where — and that she's okay. And they'll both be back tomorrow."

"Tomorrow's our last day, kids," Aunt Vera reminded them.

"It *is?* Rats!" said Anastasia. She had lost track of time.

"And tomorrow we have the video camera again. We'll take the 'Afters' and compare them with the 'Befores.' "

"Mine will really show an improvement," Bambie announced. "I've been practicing that Juliet monologue at home. And it really works better if I sort of *drape* myself over a chair. Then, see, I can hold up the vial of poison like this." She raised one arm dramatically.

123

Henry groaned.

Anastasia wasn't at all certain that her "After" tape would be any better than her "Before." Her new haircut did help, she realized. She looked less scruffy than she had. If she tried real hard, she could look right into the camera and speak distinctly. But her posture and walk were still like a giraffe's.

She was quite sure that she would never be a model. And she didn't care. She was beginning to think that she actually could be a successful bookstore owner.

"Henry," she said, when they were walking to the place where Anastasia would catch her bus and Henry her train, "even though I hate Robert Giannini — no, I mean I really don't care very much for Robert Giannini — I have to admit that I was pretty impressed when he went off to find Helen Margaret. The rest of us were just sitting there doing nothing, but old Robert, well, he was decisive. I was impressed by that."

"Me, too. I like Robert. He's okay."

Anastasia sighed. "Maybe I actually like him a little, too. I just wish he wouldn't say stuff like 'chest hair.' "

Henry laughed. "I know people who say stuff a lot worse than that. 'Chest hair,' that's *nuthin*.' "

"What was it he said he was considering for a career — metallurgy? What's metallurgy?"

Henry shrugged. "Dunno."

"Do you think someone who does metallurgy gets rich?"

Henry glared at Anastasia. "You quit planning on a rich husband, Anastasia. You're gonna get rich on your own. You and me, if we *want* husbands, fine. But we won't *need* them. Like our mothers. My mom could do just fine being a waitress, and your mom could do just fine being an artist. They got husbands cuz they *want* them. That Bambie, now maybe *she'll* need a husband. But not you and me. Got it?"

Anastasia laughed. "Okay. Got it." Then she added, "I really had fun at your house last night. I hope you'll invite me again. You won't forget me after the course ends, will you?"

"Well, shoot, how could I forget someone who's been my best friend for a whole week? And I've got your phone number."

Anastasia nodded. "And I won't forget *you*, for sure! I'll probably be seeing you on magazine covers and stuff, when you're a famous model. But I'll call you next week, before you're famous."

"Yeah," Henry said matter-of-factly. "I'll probably be on — what's that one called? *Vogue.* You gimme a year or two to get my act together, then I'll be on *Vogue.*"

"But don't forget college. Promise you'll go to college."

"Shoot, that's a hunnert years from now," Henry laughed. "My looks'll be gone by then, anyway."

A man leaning against a wall near the bus stop looked Henry up and down as the girls walked past. Then he gave a long, low, admiring whistle.

Henry whirled around and glared at him. "Stick it in your ear, turkey," she said.

* * *

125

Sitting wearily on the bus during her ride home, Anastasia thought about what Henry had said to the man. It was such an assertive thing to say. *Flagrant* — that's what it was; flagrant.

Anastasia wished she could say stuff like that. It wasn't that she couldn't pronounce the words. Heck, the words were easy. "Stick." "It." "In." "Your." "Ear." "Turkey." Each one was a word she had said a million times. But somehow, all put together, with the right inflection — and staring the person straight in the eye, the way Henry had done — well, then it took on a whole new feeling.

"Stick it in your ear, turkey," she murmured to herself, practicing. There. She had said it just right: scornfully, assertively, flagrantly.

Now if the right occasion would just come along. If someone were rude to her, the way that man had been to Henry. Surely it would happen. People were rude to Anastasia all the time.

Why, just the week before her very own father had been rude to her. He had falsely accused her of messing with his precious Billie Holiday records. And she hadn't; her brother, Sam, had been the guilty one.

Anastasia envisioned the scene. Her father had bellowed, "Anastasia Krupnik, I've told you a million times to keep your mitts off my Billie Holiday records, and you never *listen!*"

She envisioned herself looking her father straight in the eye and saying, "Stick it in your ear, turkey."

Gulp. No, that wasn't the right occasion. You couldn't say that to your own father, no matter how rude he was.

Well, what about the time — also just the week before — when she had been whispering to Sonya about nude photographs, and Mr. Earnshaw had embarrassed her in front of the whole study hall by saying, "I want to see you after class — fully clothed," with that sarcastic tone?

She pictured herself marching up to Mr. Earnshaw's desk, looking him right in the eye, and saying, "Stick it in your ear, turkey."

Thinking of it, she cringed. No. That wasn't the right occasion, either.

The bus stopped at Anastasia's corner. "Move it," the driver said angrily to the two boys getting off in front of Anastasia. One of them had dropped a package and was trying to pick it up. "I haven't got all day."

Well, *that* was sure rude. If he says anything like that to me, Anastasia thought, it will be the right occasion.

She moved forward toward the door of the bus. At the top of the steps she stumbled. She grabbed the rail to steady herself.

"Come on, come on," the bus driver grumbled. "Let's get this show on the road, sister."

Anastasia turned and looked him right in the eye.

"I'm sorry, sir," she mumbled.

She was still mad at herself when she got home. She didn't greet her parents or her brother. She dropped her jacket angrily in the back hall and stomped up the stairs to her bedroom.

Unassertive twerp, she said to herself, and slumped onto her bed.

From inside his bowl, Frank Goldfish looked out at her with his bulgy eyes. Great; she'd forgotten to feed him that morning. Anastasia sighed and tapped some fish food into the bowl. Frank swam hastily to the surface and gobbled it up. Then he came to the side of the bowl and stared at her. His mouth opened and closed. He was probably demanding a second helping.

Anastasia stared him straight in the eye.

"Stick it in your ear, turkey," she said.

Boy, *that* felt good.

Anastasia Krupnik

My Chosen Career

One of the things that I find most appealing about My Chosen Career, bookstore owner, is that you can do it sitting down, most of the time. From your sitting-down position you can reach for the phone or the cash register or even to the bookshelf to take out a book if it isn't up on a high shelf.

Therefore, Bookstore Owner is a good choice of career for people who tend to have an ungraceful walk.

You would have to get up from your sitting position in order to be assertive sometimes, like if someone wanted to return a book with coffee stains and you wanted to say something extremely rude to them. But you could just stand up and look them in the eye while you said it very distinctly. You wouldn't need to walk gracefully across the room, or anything. Then you could sit back down and watch while they slunk away, ashamed of themselves.

13

"And let's see, what else? What did I get out of this week? Well, I got a terrific haircut," Anastasia said, staring into the camera. She wasn't quite as nervous as she had been on Monday.

"And I got advice about clothes, even though I can't afford to buy them.

"And I had a lot of fun." She grinned.

"And last, but maybe most important, I made some new friends. And especially my friend Henry Peabody." Anastasia kept looking at the camera, but she could see, from the corner of her eye, Henry Peabody give her a thumbs-up sign.

"The end. Thank you."

Uncle Charley turned off the camera and nodded at her. "Good," he said.

Anastasia went back to her seat and looked around. She had been third. Bambie, as usual, had said, "Me first!" Bambie hadn't wanted to do the assignment — to talk about what they had gotten out of the course. She had insisted on doing her boring Juliet monologue again.

Afterward, when Uncle Charley had shown Bambie's "Before" and then her "After," they had all laughed. Bambie hadn't changed at all. She still looked exactly the same; her monologue had been exactly the same, with the same stupid gestures in the same places.

But Bambie didn't care. She thought she was terrific *before*. And she thought she was terrific *after*.

Then Henry had gone next. She stood self-confidently in front of the camera and spoke about her hopes for a career. Henry's appearance was not such a colossal surprise anymore, though it still threw the group into awed silence. But now she was less smart-alecky, more poised, more cheerful. It had only been a week, Anastasia realized in amazement. It was probably the best $119 Henry Peabody had ever spent.

At the end of her speech, after she said, "I'd like to thank everybody here who helped me see that I could be successful," Henry couldn't resist adding, with a big wink, "and *rich*."

Everyone applauded.

Robert Giannini and Helen Margaret were back. They were sitting beside each other, and Robert had announced that they would go before the camera last. Helen Margaret hadn't spoken to anyone, but she looked much calmer than she had the day before.

"Robert? Are you ready?" asked Uncle Charley, and Robert nodded.

He leaned his briefcase against his chair and went to stand in front of the camera. "Are you in focus? Should I start?" he asked.

"Go," said Uncle Charley.

Robert cleared his throat. "I got a lot out of this week," he said. "For one thing, my new hair style, I think, makes me look more mature."

Mature my foot, thought Anastasia. Oh, well; that was just old Robert. If he thinks he looks mature, what the heck.

"And I've also made new friends. I've known Anastasia Krupnik for a long time, but I've enjoyed meeting Bambie and Henry, and I wish them both great success in the future."

Yawn yawn yawn YAWN, thought Anastasia.

"Most especially," Robert went on, "I've gotten to know Helen Margaret Howell, who is a very special person. She and I spent the afternoon together yesterday, and we'd like to tell you about it together."

Henry nudged Anastasia, and they both watched, surprised, as Helen Margaret got up and went to stand beside Robert.

"Helen Margaret, honey," Aunt Vera said, "you don't have to do a videotape if you don't want to."

"I want to," Helen Margaret replied in a shy voice.

Robert cleared his throat again. "When I went looking for her yesterday, I finally caught a glimpse of Helen Margaret walking across the Common."

"Running," whispered Helen Margaret. "I was running."

"Well, yes, actually she was running. But I saw her and I followed her all the way down to Commonwealth Avenue. She didn't see me."

"I was crying," Helen Margaret said. "I didn't see *anything*, because I was crying."

Robert nodded. "I followed her on Commonwealth Avenue until she went into a building. I knew she didn't live there because her address was Somerville—"

Helen Margaret said, "I live with my aunt and uncle in Somerville."

"I went into the building behind her," Robert went on, "and I could see that she went into a doctor's office. It was a psych—" He turned to the girl beside him. "Do you mind if I tell them this?"

Helen Margaret smiled. "I'll tell them," she said in her quiet voice. "It was my psychiatrist's office."

Aunt Vera interrupted. "Kids, we really don't need to get into any heavy stuff here. I'm just glad that Helen Margaret's okay. The tape's long enough. Thanks, Robert and Hel—"

"No, *wait!*" Robert said angrily. "Let us finish. That's the whole trouble — people get embarrassed about other people's problems, so they don't want to know about them. And then if you don't have anybody to talk to — because they won't *listen* — then the problems *stay*. That's what a psychiatrist is *for* — to listen to people's problems."

"I'm sorry, Robert," Aunt Vera said quietly. "Go on. We're listening."

"Well, I know about it firsthand because when I was younger I went to a psychiatrist myself. My parents took me because I was a bed wetter."

Oh, no, thought Anastasia. She looked at the floor.

133

She felt awfully relieved that Helen Margaret was back and seemed to be okay, and she felt grateful to Robert for helping Helen Margaret recover from whatever had gone wrong the day before, but the last thing in the world she wanted to hear was about Robert Giannini being a bed wetter, for pete's sake. Talk about *embarrassing*.

She glanced at Henry so that they could make faces at each other. But Henry was watching Robert, listening intently.

She looked over at Bambie. And Bambie was watching Robert, too, and listening with a sympathetic look.

Nobody looked embarrassed. They looked understanding. Probably every one of them had had problems at some time, and nobody to tell them to. Anastasia knew that *she* had, for sure.

So she looked at Robert and listened. She tried to feel sympathetic instead of embarrassed. And after a moment, the embarrassment was gone.

"Well, anyway," he was saying, "that was a long time ago and I don't have that problem anymore. But I remember what it was like when other kids used to make fun of me, and I didn't have anyone I could talk to.

"So I waited for almost an hour while Helen Margaret was in the doctor's office. And I was there when she came out. I was freezing by then because I was just wearing my Harris tweed jacket — you remember that yesterday I was wearing my Harris tweed jacket with the side vents — and I was sitting on cement steps, and the jacket doesn't cover my buttocks — "

Oh, *no*. Just when Anastasia had gotten over being embarrassed, Robert Giannini had said "buttocks."

Helen Margaret started to giggle. She poked Robert. "Quit it, Robert. You're starting to sound like a jerk. Get to the point. Or let me tell the rest."

Robert looked a little insulted for a second. Then he chuckled. "Okay," he said. "You go on."

Helen Margaret took a deep breath. "The reason I live with my aunt and uncle is because my parents are dead," she said.

She looked straight ahead at the camera and talked steadily and quietly. "I used to live in Wisconsin," she said. "Last fall there was a fire in our house. My parents were both killed."

Aunt Vera gasped. "Oh, honey, I'm sorry," she said. "You don't need to go on."

"No, it's okay. I *want* to," Helen Margaret said firmly. Anastasia noticed that she was clutching Robert's hand, but her voice was very firm.

"They were both killed in the fire, along with my brother. And I was badly burned. I was in a special hospital here in Boston until last month.

"And I'm really okay now. I told Robert all about it yesterday, sitting on the steps of my doctor's building — "

"Freezing," Robert added.

"Yeah, freezing. Finally we went to Brigham's and ordered hot chocolate. And while we were there I told him about the rest. Even though I'm fine now, I still have a lot of scars. Not on my face."

135

She smiled timidly at the camera. Anastasia noticed again how perfect her pale skin was, and how sweet her smile.

"But my arms and chest and back, they were all burned. The doctors had to graft skin there. So I have scars. It's going to take me awhile to get used to that. But I guess I'll have to, because they'll always be there.

"I've never shown them to anybody, except of course the doctors. I always wear long-sleeved things so no one will see.

"The psychiatrist thought it would be a good idea for me to take this course, to help get my self-confidence back. And I was doing okay, I think. I really liked my haircut on Tuesday. And the walking — well, it was kind of silly, I thought, but I didn't really mind trying to walk like a deer.

"But yesterday — well, I'm sorry about yesterday. When I got into the dressing room, and Aunt Vera started to try to unbutton my sweater, I should have explained, but — I don't know — I couldn't. I freaked."

Bambie Browne said, "I know *exactly* how you felt. I freaked just like that once, when I was in this beauty pageant, I think it was for Junior Miss Apple Cider, and someone spilled Pepsi on my custom-made outfit — "

Everyone burst into laughter.

"Well," Bambie said huffily, "it wasn't funny."

Stick it in your ear, turkey, thought Anastasia. But she didn't say it.

"*Anyway*," Helen Margaret went on, "I'm sorry I upset everybody. I'm really okay. But I'm not ready to model that dress, not with its low neck and short sleeves. Maybe someday. But not yet."

"Dammit!" Uncle Charley bellowed suddenly. "I've run out of tape."

"That's too bad," Helen Margaret said. "I didn't have a chance to say what I got out of the course."

Aunt Vera walked over and hugged her. "Yes, you did, honey. We should pay *you* for teaching *us*."

Then she added, with a chuckle, "But don't you dare ask for your money back. It's already gone to pay the electric bill."

"I'm sorry to bother you at work," Anastasia said into the phone. She was standing in the phone booth outside McDonald's.

Barbara Page laughed. "That's okay. There's nobody in the store but me. I'm reading the new Updike novel."

"Well, I'm calling because I wanted to thank you for the books you gave Henry and me. And also because I still never did the interview, and now I'm really getting nervous because I have to write the paper this weekend, and so far all I have are twelve different beginnings and none of them are any good. So can I ask you a few questions?"

"Sure. Go ahead." '

Anastasia looked down at the list of open-ended questions she had made the night before.

"In your opinion, what kind of person makes the best bookstore owner?"

"A person who loves books," Barbara Page said.

"Right. I figured that. But don't you think, also, that it ought to be a person who likes *people*, and a person who is well organized and decisive and assertive and has a good head for business?"

"Sure," said Barbara Page.

"Great. Now, second question: what kind of training and experience does a potential bookstore owner need?"

"Gosh, I never really thought about that. When I decided to be a bookstore owner, I was pretty good at horseback riding, and I could play the cello."

"But how about a college degree, maybe in literature, and also some courses in accounting, and maybe it would help, too, to work as a clerk in a bookstore during the summers while you're young? And maybe, even, a course in modeling so that you could develop self-confidence and poise and a fashion sense?"

"Sure. Sounds good to me," said Barbara Page. "I wouldn't even put in about the cello, if I were you."

"Okay. Now this one: what are the *bad* things about being a bookstore owner?"

"None. None at all."

"Well, don't you think that maybe it could be a problem that you have to spend long hours in the store, sometimes with nobody else there?"

"But you get to *read*," Barbara Page pointed out.

Anastasia thought about that. "So that's a *good* thing, not a bad one. Okay, I'll put that down: no bad things. And the next question is what are the good things? But you already answered that. Are there any other good things?"

Barbara Page laughed. "Just think of all the interesting people I get to meet. You and Henry, for example. I would never have met you if I hadn't been a bookstore owner. Or your father. Or the senior citizens or the nursery school kids or the UPS man or old Mr. Cook up the street, who's ninety-three and likes to read books about mountain climbing, or the guy who calls me collect from the state prison and talks about books because I'm the only one he has to talk to about books —"

"He calls *collect?*"

"I don't mind."

"Well, I guess that's a special case. That's all my questions, Barbara — thank you. I can write my paper now. I'm really looking forward to writing it. But I have a confession to make."

"A lurid, explicit True Confession? Mrs. Van Gilder on Pinckney Street loves reading those."

Anastasia giggled. "No. It's only that when I started out this week, I didn't really *truly* want to be a bookstore owner. I only told Dad I did so that he'd let me come into Boston to take the modeling course. But now, you know what? After meeting you and thinking about it, I think maybe I *do*. I think I might be a really successful bookstore owner someday. I mean, I don't want to be rude or anything, but I bet I could even sell some books!"

"I'm sure you could. You're the first person to sell a volume of your father's poetry in three months."

Anastasia peered through the phone booth, across the sidewalk. "Oh, Barbara," she said, "I have to go, because I'm looking into McDonald's and Henry's there —

she's holding up her Coke toward me and acting weird."

"What do you mean, weird?"

"Well, I'm not sure. She's holding up her Coke and gesturing as if it's poison or something—oh, no!" Anastasia started to laugh. "She's doing a scene from *Romeo and Juliet!*"

"I did it," Anastasia announced to her parents on Sunday afternoon. "I wrote my paper for school. 'My Chosen Career.' And I'm sure I'll get an A. But I still have one problem."

"What's that?" her father asked, looking up from the *New York Times* crossword puzzle.

"I don't know what I'll name my bookstore. Barbara Page was so lucky, having just the right name. But *Krupnik?* How can you call a bookstore '*Krupniks*'?"

"Barbara Page married her name," Dr. Krupnik pointed out. "She didn't start out with the name Page."

"Yeah, I know. But if I decide to get married when I'm older, I *already* have a whole long list of stuff to look for in a husband, and—"

"Really?" Her mother looked up from her section of the newspaper with interest. "Like what?"

"Sense of humor. Tall. Not allergic to dogs." Anastasia glared for a moment at her father, who was allergic to dogs, even though she knew it wasn't his fault. "Stuff like that. But now I have to add: right name for bookstore. And I can't even think of one, since Page is already taken."

"Goodness," said Mrs. Krupnik, looking back down at the paper, "that *is* a problem. You may have to spend your entire teenage years looking for someone named Harold Volume who isn't allergic to dogs, and then persuading him to marry you so that you can call your bookstore 'Volumes.' "

"I once knew a guy in the army who was named Ralph Plott," Dr. Krupnik said. "Would that do? It had two 't's, but I suppose you could take off one 't' and call your bookstore 'Plots.' Or you could sell cemeteries."

Anastasia made a face. "You guys aren't taking me seriously. May I use your typewriter, Dad? I want to type my paper."

He nodded, and she headed for the study. Behind her, she could hear her mother murmer, "There was a girl in my class in art school, Myron, whose name was Booky. It really was. Alexandra Booky. I wonder if that would be an appropriate name for a bookst — "

Anastasia closed the door to the study. She sat down at her father's big desk and looked around the room — her very favorite room in their house. The walls were lined with shelves and the shelves were filled with books. She was surrounded by books, and not only by books but by pages, sentences, paragraphs, plots, commas, periods, poems, drawings, boxed sets, first editions, paperbacks, portfolios. . . .

She sighed. It was a sigh of contentment, not worry. She had plenty of time, and she would find the right name for her bookstore someday. For now, it was enough

141

that she had had a terrific week and had written a terrific paper. Carefully she rolled a sheet of paper into the typewriter and began to type her title.

MMY ChoXSEN carEER

Maybe, Anastasia thought gloomily, as she crumpled that piece of paper and inserted another into the typewriter, she shouldn't have spent the week studying modeling. Maybe she should have taken a typing course.